MIRREN

THE SCOTTISH LIONS

ANNE GREGOR

All rights reserved.

No part of this publication may be sold, copied, distributed, reproduced or transmitted in any form or by any means, mechanical or digital, including photocopying and recording or by any information storage and retrieval system without the prior written permission of both the publisher, Oliver Heber Books and the author, Anne Gregor, except in the case of brief quotations embodied in critical articles and reviews.

NO AI TRAINING: Without in any way limiting the author's [and publisher's] exclusive rights under copyright, any use of this publication to "train" generative artificial intelligence (AI) technologies and/or large language models to generate text, or any other medium, is expressly prohibited. The author reserves all rights to license uses of this work for the training and development of any generative AI and/or large language models.

PUBLISHER'S NOTE: This is a work of fiction. Names, characters, places, and incidents either are the product of the author's imagination or are used fictitiously. Any resemblance to actual persons, living or dead, business establishments, events, or locales is entirely coincidental.

Mirren Copyright 2025 © Anne Gregor

Cover art by Dar Albert at Wicked Smart Designs

Published by Oliver-Heber Books

0 9 8 7 6 5 4 3 2 1

1

FOURTEEN YEARS EARLIER—EDINBURGH,
SCOTLAND

F inn tried to calm the rising panic thumping through his chest. He was two hours late getting off work, making him two hours late to meet his sister, Fiona. She would wait in the cemetery across from their house until he got home.

She would not enter their home without him.

"She better not," he huffed, but his worry was increasing with every minute that ticked by. He regretted for the millionth time that he couldn't afford cell phones.

He sped up from a fast walk to a jog, leaving the busy city's center behind. One mile—just one mile—until he could breathe easier again. He only needed to see that his sister was safe. His other half. His twin. They watched out for each other, of course, but he was—had always been—his sister's protector.

He had a great job for a high school student. He was able to keep himself and his sister from starving with enough money left over for a few secondhand clothes and shoes. With his recent raise, he hoped to save up enough for some art paper and pencils.

They each loved to draw, but where she thrived on recreating busy city scenes, he dreamed of one day creating with metal. As children, they'd spent hours dreaming about selling their art someday.

He used his fingers to create imaginary images on any surface or clouds in the sky and could be satisfied with seeing his creations come to life in his mind's eye. Fiona said her imagination wasn't as good as his and that paper was better than sunny skies. She would always laugh and act like she was only joking. She wasn't but was too kind to ever complain about what they didn't have. He was determined that their lives would be better.

He'd started off as a dishwasher for an upscale pizzeria when he was fourteen. The owner had to be the coolest boss ever. Sadie Gold was a blonde, brash American who enjoyed nothing so much as arguing with her Italian husband and head chef, Alex, playing League of Legends, and creating unique pizza combinations for her husband to try.

With Alex's and Sadie's encouragement and training, he could toss pizza dough like a pro. Golden Pizzeria & Cocktails had received awards every year since opening six years ago.

They had always been so good to Finn, which was why he hadn't minded staying late to help with an anniversary party. He hadn't expected it to be that late though...

No matter how many times he told himself his sister would follow the rules, he knew patience wasn't her best quality. The two of them had come up with an after-school schedule that had worked to keep them safe for the past year.

They were both in a work-release school program, so they got out at one in the afternoon every day. They had good enough grades to be released before that, but Finn needed them to stay past lunch. It was the only meal they got for the day during the week. Weekends were when his earnings came in handy to buy staple food items, usually from the day-old bin or the shelves of expired boxes, jars, and cans.

All of Fiona's paycheck went toward paying rent on the shitty one-bedroom flat they were forced to share with their deadbeat sperm donor. The apartment complex had to be one of the oldest and most rundown in all of Scotland. The floor's linoleum wasn't just cracked but missing in high-traffic areas, which was pretty much the entire flat since it was the size of a postcard.

Their dad got the shoebox-sized bedroom. Finn had asked whether Fiona could have the room for the small bit of privacy it would afford her when she turned thirteen. He'd gotten a black eye and bruised ribs for his trouble. He had hung up an old sheet from the low, sagging ceiling where her pallet sat in the living room instead. It gave his sister at least a modicum of privacy to store her tampons and whatnot since the bathroom had no cabinets or drawers.

Their dad was a mean drunk—had been for as long as Finn could remember. Finn couldn't recall ever seeing his softspoken mother without bruises before she died, when her children were barely seven. He'd always wondered why she hadn't run away. He'd never been brave enough to ask.

He and Fiona had been planning to leave home the moment they graduated and vowed to never look back. They'd tried to find their own room in the city, but no one would rent to teenagers. Their dad rarely worked, but when he managed to sober up, he'd take the odd job here and there. He would spend every dime he earned on cheap whisky.

Finn could take the slaps, punches, and derogatory slurs. That was simply how things were. What he couldn't take was the way his dad had started eyeing Fiona when he was drunk and in a mood to fight. He would watch her, not saying anything but tracking her with his eyes, even after she would slip behind her sheet divider.

A year ago, their dad had beaten him worse than normal. He'd kept yelling at Fi that she was a whore to bring another man into the house. He'd called her "Brenda."

"Brenda" had been their mother's name.

Neither Finn nor his sister wanted to voice what that might mean for Fiona. They knew their dad couldn't ever be allowed to be near his daughter without Finn present, which was why their current safety protocols had been established.

Showers were done quickly. Fiona would have to stay in the bathroom and turn her back while he showered or used the toilet. He would stand outside the door to guard her privacy while she took her turn.

They walked to school together and left together. Finn escorted his sister to her after-school job at a facility for the elderly even though it was out of his way. Neither of them wanted to chance their dad finding her unprotected. There was no help for her walking home alone, as she got off an hour and a half before Finn, but she took a roundabout route home and sneaked into a cemetery that was only two blocks from their flat. Years ago, they had enjoyed playing under one of the small private mausoleums that had a slight covered stoop in the front.

She would settle in a corner that was partially shielded by bushes and work on homework or read until he got off work and could walk her home. There, they hid a box containing an old blanket and a camping lantern that ran on batteries—another expense but a necessary one.

Finn stumbled over the cemetery's threshold, almost smacking his knee on the heavy iron of the filigreed gate that always sat partially open.

He didn't call out, not wanting to draw a passerby's attention. Not that anyone was likely to be roaming around that old cemetery in the misty rain. His clothes and light jacket were past damp, and the temperature had dropped enough to make his body uncomfortably clammy after the exertion of his jog.

There was no light. "Damn it, Fi." She wasn't there. "You're such a baby about the cold." He muttered under his breath as he turned to leave the way he'd come. Since the weather was crap, Fiona would have chosen to wait at one of the all-night internet cafés that the uni students frequented.

He would have liked her to always wait there, but they couldn't afford to spend money on coffee five days a week—six if they were able to pick up work shifts on Saturday. Fiona had said some of the waitresses were kind about her not buying anything, but there were a few that gave her a hard time because they wouldn't make tips off her table.

Cursing himself for not having gone there first, he jogged the two blocks to Brick Room. Fiona had put in an application at Brick last week. Maybe she would greet him with the good news that they'd hired her. The café offered a longer shift than she currently worked. Working there would mean taking a pay cut, but working later would be safer than waiting for Finn all the time.

The Brick was packed, the interior's yellow glow outlining dozens of patrons. He pulled the old brass door handle and stepped inside. Warmth instantly flowed around his chilled body. He scanned the tables, not catching sight of his sister. There were about a dozen boys and girls clacking away on laptop keys, but none of them had Fiona's dark-auburn hair, the match to his own ruddy mess.

He didn't need the visual confirmation that she wasn't there. He and Fiona could always feel when the other was close. Finn knew it wasn't that way with all twins, and he always wondered whether they had been born with the connection or it had grown out of necessity.

He caught sight of Marie, one of the nicer waitresses who didn't mind pretending to her boss that Fiona was a paying customer. He approached close enough to catch her eye, bobbing his head slightly to let her know he needed to speak to her.

"Hey, Finn," she said and smiled as she met him by one of the empty tables.

"Hey, Marie. Have you seen Fi tonight?" He didn't like the brief look of concern that flashed across the woman's round cheeks.

"She was here, but that had to be at least three hours ago. She left with...she called him 'Dad.'"

Finn spun around and headed for the exit. Marie called out behind him, "He called her 'Brenda.' I asked if she was okay, Finn, and she said it was okay. I should have insisted..."

Finn's body shuddered in horror. "Not your fault." He got out the reassurance through his choked throat as he shoved open the Brick's door and ran.

FINN BURST through the flat's thin, grimy door, breaking the decades-old locking chain. The scene that greeted him on the living room floor would haunt him the rest of his days. Their father was lying on his back, snoring softly and sporting a giant bump on the side of his forehead, dried blood crusting its edges.

His pants were shoved around his ankles, his heavy boots keeping them from going any lower. His dick was lying flaccid against his thigh—smeared with blood.

A moan welled deep in Finn's throat as he finally allowed himself to look at his sister. Her eyes were wide and unblinking as she watched him. She was kneeling on bare legs, surrounded by broken glass and whisky, which was dripping slowly through the cracks in the linoleum.

Her shirt was torn, and bruises were marring her neck and chest—shaking hands were gripping her torn jeans against her crotch.

"Finn."

That was all she said.

2

PRESENT DAY, SMITH GALLERY—EDINBURGH, SCOTLAND

Who in the hell does this absolute dickhead think he is? Mirren was struggling to keep her face neutral, but who was she kidding? Subtlety wasn't her strong suit, and she knew her expression was screaming, "Asshole."

When Mr. Ruggedly Handsome had shown up with one of the gallery's artists, she'd secretly hoped they weren't together... *together* together to be exact. She'd been admiring how the sun's rays slanting through the unshuttered front windows highlighted hints of red in his warm-brown hair and beard, but she'd ditched her admiring inspection when he had decided to speak.

Mirren was about to introduce herself to the woman at his side, Fiona Campbell, the highly talented painter whom, until that moment, Mirren hadn't spoken to or laid eyes on. All of their communication was through email, but it was clear Fiona had quite a sense of humor, and she'd been looking forward to that meeting not only because Ms. Campbell was one of the gallery's most favored artists.

Mirren extended her hand out to shake Fiona's. "It's so good to finally meet y—" Before she could finish, the man, who was clearly all looks and zero manners, interrupted.

9

"Where did you get that jewelry?"

Attempting to ignore how the steely timbre of his voice sent tingles from her throat to her fingers, she chose to focus on his rudeness. Mirren would have typically answered immediately and without an ounce of hesitation, but his...tone... Demanding tones tended not to sit well with her.

Few men had that level of intensity. Her father, Thomas MacGregor, was one of them. Her Uncle Coll could be intense when a situation called for it. Hugh O'Faolain, a retired oil mogul from Oklahoma who was good friends with her parents, was definitely intense.

Their wives always said that men like that couldn't help but evoke strong reactions—good, bad, and very good. Josephine, Mirren's stepmom, often said that she wanted to kiss or smack her husband every time he opened his mouth.

The man standing in front of Mirren right then would make the smack list.

If their meeting was to stay on track, she was going to have to relent. "It was a gift." Mirren had to force the words through her clenched teeth.

"What's your name?"

Mirren had never wanted to whack someone more and felt a snarl working its way up her throat. "I was about to give it when you interrupted." She left off "rudely," but it was implied.

Fiona touched the man's arm to get his attention before signing, "You're being rude. Stop it now."

Mirren hadn't known the artist was deaf. She was pleased that her BSL was excellent. Her Uncle Coll and Aunt Catriona's daughter, Blair, had been born deaf. Their whole family and many of their friends had learned sign language. Mirren had to fight really hard not to smile at Fiona's words.

The man ignored Fiona. *Shocking.*

Instead, he asked, "Where was the necklace purchased?" which was quickly followed by, "Do you have the entire set?"

Mirren was surprised that he knew it was a set. It was a good thing neither of her bosses was in to witness the bizarre interrogation. Kain and Lillias Smith were siblings from a wealthy London family. All the Smiths were art collectors. Kain and Lillias just chose to make money at it and had galleries all over the world.

Mirren managed the Edinburgh store and was often praised for her skill at handling the various personality quirks of the artists they managed. It also didn't hurt that the store's sales had skyrocketed since she'd taken over last year.

Her family always said she could sell a lactose-intolerant man a monthly subscription for ice cream. They weren't wrong. Finding the perfect painting for her clients and then encouraging them to loosen their purse strings was a thrill that never got old.

Fiona tugged on the man's sleeve with more force, signing, "Brother. Enough."

Ahh, siblings, then. If the man's face wasn't flexing with impatience, Mirren supposed she could have seen a resemblance. She should have noted the hair, but, in her defense, they lived in Scotland, where every conceivable shade of red hair could be found.

Mirren decided to give the man what he wanted. Perhaps he would leave the store once his curiosity was assuaged. How unfair that such a smoke show had the personality of a potato.

"My name is Mirren Mòr MacGregor-Morrow. And, yes, I'm aware it has a surplus of *Ms*. Thankfully, I'm partial to the letter. Now"—Mirren clasped her hands at her waist to quell the urge to poke him in the chest—"I've already said it was a gift, and yes, I have the entire set purchased from a jewelry store in

Inverness." Ignoring the man's glare, she turned to his sister, who was trying and failing to hide a smile.

Mirren chose not to give away that she could sign. Fiona was clearly adept at reading lips, so she'd keep the secret a little longer. "I was hoping you might be up for a semiprofessional lunch, Ms. Campbell."

The artist quickly signed, "Please call me 'Fiona.'"

Grumpykins barked, "Call her 'Fiona.'"

Refusing to give the man one more second of her time, she ignored him. "Then I insist you call me 'Mirren.'" Fiona smiled and nodded. "The King's Wark has my favorite crab cocktail and whisky." Mirren grinned. "Give me a second to pop in the back office to let my assistant, Lindy, know I'll be out for a while. Does your..." she hesitated, wanting to call the silent man she had been ignoring "dickhead" but settling for "friend have errands he would like to attend to?"

Mirren felt more than saw his body stiffen up. *Mirren: one. Asswipe: zero.* Fiona quickly began typing a response on her phone, but her brother interrupted again. He seemed to have quite a talent for it.

"I'm her brother, and I will be joining you. Surely, you can't have missed that my sister doesn't speak. I help her communicate."

It was all said in his patented defensive tone, but Mirren didn't miss the sideways glance he sent Fiona and the brief touch of his index finger to her hand. Was he reassuring himself or his sister?

Fiona signed, "I am quite capable of having a conversation without your help." She frowned. "You needn't come."

Grumpy signed back, "She looks like a child barely capable of communication. We don't even know why she wanted to meet with you. It could be to reduce your fee. Gallery owners are all sharks. We should just go back to selling them ourselves."

Mirren wasn't sure what was more annoying, that he thought she looked childlike or that he thought she was a cheat. His testicles were calling to the pointy toe of her kitten heel. Ignoring their exchange, she said, "That's settled then. I'm thrilled you'll be able to join us." She made sure he knew what a lie that was.

"Might I be blessed with knowing your name? Or are you the only one allowed to ask questions and demand answers?" Mirren was satisfied when she saw the slight pinkening of his sharp cheekbones above his full, bushy beard. She wasn't too salty to admit—only to herself—that it was a lovely beard.

"Finn Campbell."

3

———————

M. *MacGregor, Scotland.* The name matched the jewelry store's registry. Finn had thought about finding M. MacGregor several times over the years as he had become more successful. He'd always dreamed of buying the set back.

The sassy brunette glaring at him didn't deserve his bad mood. He hated traveling to Edinburgh. He hated going anywhere near the city he'd fled all those years ago. He wouldn't have allowed his sister anywhere near its borders had he not received a notice that their father had died last year.

Burned to ashes was a better fate than the bastard had deserved. The only decent thing their dad had ever done was to never try to contact his children. The night when Fiona had been violated by her own father and they'd run, Finn had left a note.

Never try to find us.
If we ever see your face...ever...I will call the police and tell them what you did.
Rot in hell, you piece of shit.
The day you die will be the best day of my life.

He must have believed Finn's threat, and he should have. He'd meant every quickly scribbled word.

He'd hated to do it when Fiona was clearly in shock, but Finn had forced her to her feet and told her to use the restroom and shower. He may have been a sixteen-year-old virgin, but even he had known that the longer a man's seed stayed inside a woman, the better chance it had to take root.

Fiona had said nothing, but she had followed his instructions. While she'd taken care of herself, he'd packed all their belongings into two duffels, packing what little food he'd had hidden away and the eighty-two pounds from his old man's wallet. Finn had had the forethought to also grab the piece of shit's cell phone. He'd known the password was his father's birthday; the prick had always put himself first.

Their mother had had one cantankerous cousin who'd lived a hermit's life in the Orkney Islands north of Scotland. St Margaret's Hope had become his and Fiona's healing sanctuary. Aila had hated children and had hated interruptions to her quiet world more, but she'd let the two sixteen-year-olds make a home for themselves in the snug barn behind her house.

Finn had used their dad's phone to withdraw himself and his sister from school and sign them up for homeschooling. He'd withdrawn two thousand pounds from their dad's bank account —the bastard had been holding out on them—and left him with a measly nineteen pounds.

When Aila had died from untreated breast cancer three years after they'd arrived on her doorstep, he and Fiona had been nineteen and, thankfully, legal adults. Incredibly, Aila had left her property to him and Fi. They'd stayed living in the barn, turning Aila's wee cottage into an art studio. Oil painting for his sister and jewelry design for him. As he had built a name for himself, he'd been able to build his own modest forge.

An Unkindness of Ravens had been his first one-of-a-kind

set. He'd held on to it for years before letting it go out into the world. That set had spoken to him, and he hadn't wanted to part from it. He'd started dreaming of the design when he was fifteen and still sleeping on their old flat's miserable excuse for a couch. Ravens had flitted through his mind for months. He'd wished a million or more times to be one of those stoic birds able to fly above the stinky shit of humans.

He would have kept the collection had Fiona not been diagnosed with cervical cancer. Her medical bills had crushed them for years. Selling the set four years ago had paid for the last of the hospital debt that they'd been making payments on for six years already.

She hadn't told Finn about her bleeding for months. When she'd finally fessed up, he'd forced her to the doctor... The news had been doubly horrific since cervical cancer was spread through sexual intercourse.

She'd had only one partner.

Christ, he remembered that day. He would have sold everything he'd had to save her. It had been a blessing that she'd chosen to start therapy and begin to deal with her trauma years before. Finn had been so afraid that the cancer, specifically the cause of the cancer, would set back her progress.

It had taken Fiona seven years to speak out loud to him. Her selective mutism had hurt them both. Every day, she'd been reminded about what had been done to her, and each of those days, he'd been reminded that he had failed to protect his sister.

It had been his idea to learn sign language so they could use it when they were in public, drawing much less unwanted attention. When he had asked her whether she would try to speak to someone besides him, she had always said she wasn't ready. He had known it was because she didn't want anyone to get too close—that she was always worried that someone would find out her secret.

Fiona had started to venture out on her own more over the past several months and had even let him take her out for a fun evening in Inverness to celebrate their thirtieth birthdays. It was why when she'd wanted to travel to Edinburgh, he'd complained about it, but deep down, he had known venturing out of their St Margaret's Hope bubble was the best therapy.

She'd been smiling more and even laughing. She loved reading Miss MacGregor's emails to him. Finn could admit the young woman was witty.

Having met her in person, he could also admit that she was more than witty; she was brash, direct, stubborn...beautiful. Seeing his tiny gold raven resting against the smooth skin of her neck had thrown him. He couldn't believe she owned the entire set. He *wouldn't* believe it until he saw the collection with his own eyes.

At that moment, there they were seated on tall chairs, cozied up to a table and ordering drinks and appetizers. It was easier to pretend he hadn't been an ass at the gallery by staying mostly silent. Well, except for translating for his sister.

Mirren was bubbly. Her infectious smile had already spread to Fiona, and her witty observations had caused his lips to twitch a time or two. He caught himself ogling her soft, wavy brown hair and how it fell to just below her shoulders, a lovely frame for her heart-shaped face and sparkling light-brown eyes.

It was a shame that she was so young, and, of course, there was the fact that she disliked him. Forcing his gaze from her, he quickly signed to Fiona, "Ask the brat if you can see the raven collection."

"No, and she is wonderful. I think you think she is too since you're staring at her so much. Oh, and wipe the drool off your chin, weirdo," she signed back.

Ouch. Fiona wasn't playing that day. He wanted to laugh at her feistiness since, normally, he would describe her personality as mellow and nonconfrontational. Mirren coughed delicately into her hand before taking another sip of her Glenmorangie 18. The wee witch had good taste in spirits.

Mirren set her drink down and folded her hands on the table in front of her. "Since I asked you to come to Edinburgh, Fiona, and this *is* supposed to be something of a working lunch, I'll get to the meat of my proposal."

His sister smiled with encouragement and nodded once in agreement. Finn tensed. That "proposal" had been bothering him for the past week ever since Fiona had read him the email. He liked things as they were and wasn't a big fan of change. What he really disliked was his sister having ties to Edinburgh again.

Life had been easier before they'd both "made it" in the art world. Fiona's fame was on the rise, and his jewelry had been coveted for years. His sister had once merely driven to cities to take city street reference pictures before driving straight home. More and more lately, she'd been lingering in those cities. Popping into a boutique or finding unique eateries to dine in— by herself.

Watching his sister step out from her hermitage had forced him to realize that he had been isolating himself right along with her. He'd lamented his life being upended because of what had happened to his sister, which, in turn, had fed his guilt because such thoughts were selfish and should be beneath him.

The past several years, though, had found him more comfortable and satisfied with his life.

He would never leave his sister's side, but it appeared she might be leaving his.

Mirren continued, intruding into his dark thoughts. "I know you live hours from here in what must be a picturesque but... umm..."—she appeared to be struggling for an unoffensive adjective—"horrifically boring village..."

No beating about the bush for that one.

"My point is you have to travel hours to find subjects that you wish to paint. I propose—and I've already run this idea by my bosses—that you commit to living here in Edinburgh for at least a year."

"The hell she will," Finn interjected. The low volume of his denial didn't make his objection less powerful. He could hear the deep warning in his voice, and so could his sister, who immediately placed her hand on his forearm. Mirren, of course, just raised her brows.

"Continue, Mirren. Please," Fiona signed, and he was forced to repeat it, but he left off the "please."

"You're very talented at interrupting and throwing mantrums, aren't you, Mr. Campbell?"

Finn felt his face flush in embarrassment. It seemed he was doomed to make only bad impressions.

"As I was saying, commit to a year. Embrace the city, its streets, and eclectic people. The Scottish National Gallery of Modern Art is accepting entries in all genres of art over the next year. There will be winners in several categories, and those winners will receive a yearlong exhibition in Modern One's building.

"A year, Fiona. It would mean fame for the chosen artists. Fame for their lifetime and after." Mirren sat back in her chair and watched Fiona intently.

His sister signed, "I would never be chosen for something so prestigious."

Finn could see his sister was reeling from the offer. She looked skeptical and shaken. There was also yearning in her widened eyes and parted lips. He signed her misgivings even though he didn't want to.

"You're wrong. I'm young, I know, but I'm brilliant at spotting talent—the best of the best." She didn't appear to be bragging, just stating a fact. "You were on my radar from my first day on the job. Your paintings make people feel, Fiona. Your art stops people on the sidewalk, from powerful men to bitchy old money wives and even your average, everyday men and women.

"When I say I believe you have a chance at this, Fiona, I fucking mean it. My stepmother's mother bought me a ginormous three-story country house—Mary O'Connor overkills everything. I'm not even embarrassed anymore to say I have a live-in housekeeper who even cooks some of my meals. There are several bedrooms with an en suite bathroom and a chef's kitchen. You would be able to take over several rooms for living and painting.

"Mary swore she bought it with my extended family in mind, thinking they'd stay with me when they visit, but none of them ever do, preferring hotels. I swear it's because they have noisy sex, like mating Canadian moose, and don't want to offend my delicate ears.

"I suppose it could be my play-by-play comments about their sexcapades making them leery, but hey, you play, you pay. Right?"

Mirren looked so deadpan serious that Finn had to fight choking on the dark ale he'd just swallowed. His sister's cheeks pinkened, and her shoulders were shaking with mirth. Fiona looked at him. She didn't need his approval, but wanting her brother's opinion after thirty years of seeking it was a hard habit to break.

She simply signed his name. "Finn?"

"Fi." He shook his head, as overwhelmed at the changes as she. "I know you have what it takes to win, but...we fled Edinburgh fourteen years ago," Finn signed without speaking out loud. "I don't like you being—"

Mirren interrupted him that time. "Stop talking."

4

The brother and sister were about to exchange personal information, believing Mirren didn't understand sign. It had started off as a way to see what inventive and obnoxious slurs Finn Campbell would throw her way, but she refused to be privy to a private conversation, which would clearly be a sensitive one if their serious faces were anything to go by.

"I should have mentioned that I know BSL. I apologize, but I wanted to stop you from saying something personal in front of me. Even though I am just a child hell-bent on screwing you over, Fiona"—Mirren winked her way—"I draw the line at deceit and thievery."

"Jesus Christ." Mirren heard Finn mutter.

Mirren started rapidly signing and speaking aloud for the Campbells. "I have a three-year-old cousin who was born deaf. We all learned BSL. Blair is doing really well with speech therapy. She isn't a candidate for a cochlear implant, but her parents didn't cry over it, so no one else did either. My wee cousin is perfect just the way she is.

"I am sorry for not letting you know the minute I realized you were deaf. In my defense, your brother is a bit of an ass, but

I don't hold him against you." Mirren reveled in Finn's glower. However, Fiona looked pensive, and that did not make her happy.

Mirren placed her fingers close to Fiona's and tapped her knuckles to get her attention. "I hope you know that I would never make light of deafness, but my family just doesn't see it as a disability."

Fiona grimaced, quickly signing, "Ignore me, Mirren. I'm thrilled you know how to sign. My...well, my..."—Finn looked sharply at his sister but didn't say a word—"situation...I wasn't born deaf. I do agree, though, that my twin can be an ass."

Mirren waved away the uncomfortable past few minutes and asked, "What do you think? Of my proposal, that is?"

"I'm terrified," Fiona answered honestly. "Intrigued. Excited." She grinned at her brother before adding, "But I don't think I'm the only Campbell that should present the Scottish National Gallery of Modern Art with an entry."

"Enough, Fi." Finn choked out, not bothering to sign. The hairless parts of his face burned crimson.

Mirren was suddenly very curious. Was his reaction one of embarrassment or anger? His sister didn't look bothered by his warning.

"Consider me intrigued, Mr. Campbell. Are you a painter as well?"

"I am not. Ignore Fiona—she excels at being a brat."

Undeterred, Fiona quickly signed, "He's become quite a famous jeweler and metal sculptor. He is the genius behind your *An Unkindness of Ravens*."

Mirren was speechless...shocked as she touched the small gold raven at her neck. *This...this butthole is an exceptional talent?* Mirren couldn't imagine what his sculptures must look like, what with all of the man's pent-up aggression. She glanced at Finn's stony face. He was trying to contain his frustration and failing horribly.

Revelations aside, Mirren wondered why he was so persnickety about seeing his jewelry being worn. That was the whole point of his art, after all. It didn't make any sense, so she did what she always did and simply asked.

"I get it was quite a coincidence seeing your jewelry on me, but why were you so tweaked out about seeing someone wearing one of your pieces?" When it became clear that he wasn't going to answer, his sister did it for him.

Fiona placed her hand on Finn's shoulder and patted, not so much chagrined but subdued. "My brother isn't big on sharing," she started.

"I hope my face shows the surprise that my body hasn't mustered." Mirren got a quick smile from the other woman before she continued.

"I had cancer several years ago. Neither Finn nor I had insurance at the time. We spent years paying off the hospital debt. My brother had never planned on selling the *Unkindness*, but he surprised me by paying off the rest of my debt with the commission. I was furious with him, of course, but he's always been stubborn."

With every word Fiona signed, it became clear that the brother and sister sitting before her did not have a family. At least not one they could count on. Mirren was overly blessed with her own family; she forgot that many were not as fortunate.

"I'm thrilled that the set is in your hands, Mirren. That makes me happier than you can imagine. I bet my brother feels the same way. He's just having a hard time showing it. He's sensitive about the ravens because he started imagining those designs when he was just a young teenager," Fiona confessed.

Another tug on Mirren's heartstrings. "Do you still have your original sketches, Mr. Campbell?"

Fiona answered for him. Mirren got the impression that the twins finished each other's thoughts more often than not.

"No way," Fiona signed, smiling fondly at her brother, "we couldn't afford paper back then. Finn's imagination is so incredible that he could squiggle in the air with his finger and commit the designs to memory. He's always been the bigger talent of the two of us, and don't let him tell you different."

"Ignore her, Miss MacGregor. She's clearly forgotten who she's speaking for. Not that you've offered, but I am not interested in leaving our home." He reluctantly added, "But she can make her own decision."

The wide smile on Fiona's face withered. Mirren felt her spirits plummet as the other woman nodded in acceptance. She was missing...something. Rarely did Mirren feel like the odd man out, but at that moment, she felt every bit her age and out of her depth.

She didn't care for that feeling at all. The blame, of course, lay at Finn Campbell's large work-boot-clad feet. Sitting on the sidelines wasn't a part of Mirren's DNA, but before she could reprimand the bane of her current existence, Fiona signed.

"Forgive me, Brother. Every word I said is true. You are brilliant, but I understand not wanting to go through the upheaval of moving. I was being..."

Fiona didn't finish saying what she thought she was being. Mirren flashed Finn a look that showed him just what she thought of him stomping on his sister's spark. "I understand you have reservations, Fiona, but I know once you're here and settled, they'll all fly out the window. Your talent deserves every inspiration that would surround you here.

"The museum exhibit—that I know you can win—would be the ultimate payoff. Plus, think of how crazy Smith Gallery's patrons would go over the Edinburgh scenes." Mirren could tell before Fiona answered, from her soft smile and hunched, defeated shoulders, what her answer would be.

"Your confidence in me is so, so lovely to hear, but I will be staying in St Margaret's Hope with my brother."

Mirren could tell Fiona's mind would not change. At least not that day. She was frustrated but knew success was never without setbacks.

"I respect your decision. I'm disappointed and won't pretend to understand, but I respect it. I will hold the spot in my home for two weeks before I offer this opportunity to my second choice."

Opening the satchel hanging from her chair, she pulled out a one-page contract and slid it over the scarred and pitted tabletop to Fiona.

"This is the second reason, though not nearly as exciting as the first, that I asked you to make the drive. This contract," Mirren tapped the paper, "states that Smith will increase your percentage from fifty percent to sixty-five."

Fiona looked dumbstruck, while Finn looked like a man who wished he could take back the shark comment.

Fiona looked up from reading the contract with wide eyes. "But you'll make less commission. This isn't necessary. You don't need to do this."

"Of course I do. You're worth it. I imagine you'll start getting offers from other galleries to change teams. I can't believe you haven't already." Her blush gave her away. "Ahh, you have."

Fiona gave her brother a rueful look. He must not have known about the offers. She barely kept her smirk undercover. Barely.

"I'm loyal, Mirren. I always have been. I made a contract with you, and I'll damn well keep it."

That made Mirren's heart swell. Her instincts had proven to

be on point with that woman. Fiona signed the contract without further comment and pushed it back across the table.

Mirren shoved the paper back in her satchel. "Before I head back to work, I want to share a bit of my family history that may ease your mind. My mother got pregnant with me at uni when she was twenty. Her boyfriend, a young professor at the university, was given a job opportunity in the States.

"Mom had never been farther than a few hours from her family's farm outside Inverness. Her parents were shit, and my mother and her brother were very close because of it. Not seeing Uncle Coll...well, she couldn't imagine it, she said. She broke up with her boyfriend. He moved, and a few weeks later, Mom found out she was pregnant.

"She worked up the courage to call him, but before she could tell him she was pregnant and, more importantly, that she regretted not going with him and that she still loved him, he tried to hurt her like she'd hurt him and told her he loved his new job and was seeing someone he really liked.

"She never told him. Her parents would have disowned her if she had fessed up, and her dream of going to college would have had to be put on hold or permanently forgotten. Desperate, she called her brother's best friend, who was also her best friend growing up, and begged Thomas MacGregor to marry her and say the baby was his."

Mirren almost grinned when she noticed the siblings had leaned forward, arms on the table, and were listening intently to the tale.

"She regretted it instantly and told him she'd changed her mind. Dad has more love and honor in one of his fingers than most men do in their entire body. They did marry. I had the two best parents raising me a kid could hope for.

"When I was sixteen, my mother was diagnosed with breast cancer." Fiona winced and reached over to squeeze Mirren's hand. Cancer sucked. "Mom made some big changes in her life. She and Dad had lived platonically their whole marriage. They had been more siblings to one another for so long, neither wanted more." At the Campbells' raised brows of shock, Mirren chuckled.

"Yeah. Let sixteen years of Platonicville sink in. Not for Dad, of course. He was in the Royal Marines and later started a security firm that took him from home often. He had opportunities to meet women. Mom, on the other hand, lived in the same small town where she'd grown up and was a schoolteacher. Openly cheating on your husband would have been a big no-no. Not to mention how her priggish parents would have reacted.

"Cancer happened, and Mom surprised Dad with divorce papers. The love of Dad's life, who had broken up with him when she'd found out he was married and had a teenager—that's a whole other story but a goodie—well, Josephine, who's now my stepmother, got my mom into the best cancer facility in France. Josephine's mother, Mary, actually pulled that one off. She's the lovely woman who bought my house, by the way. I only put in these asides in case you guys weren't confused enough.

"There are a million other side stories to amuse you with, but I won't. Not today, at least." Mirren laughed. "Suffice it to say, Mom kicked cancer's ass, as you did, Fiona. She did divorce my dad. Dad married Josephine, who happens to be the incredible woman who bought your ravens for me, Mr. Campbell."

"Finn." Finn crossed his arms over his chest and glared at her. Perhaps he meant for Mirren to call him "Finn," but his asshole accent was hard to decipher. What a bear.

"Anyway. Mom never stopped loving my dad, my birth father, and I did a bit of sleuthing and reached out. You can imagine. It was all shock and awe and grumbles and tears. They got married and gave me a little sister, Margaret. She's three.

Dad and Jo also gave me a sister. Gray is four. Being an aunt is brilliant.

"All that backstory was to say that the decision for you not to move here isn't right or wrong. It's just a choice, and maybe, like for my Mom, even better things are waiting for you later.

"I do hope you change your mind, Fiona, but even if you don't, it won't matter. Your art will continue to speak to the world. You don't need a voice to be heard." With that, she dropped several pounds on the table to pay for their drinks and appetizers and left the pub with a spring in her step. After all, she was a MacGregor and setbacks didn't detour them. They only made them more determined.

5

____

As she slowly turned in a small, slow circle, the scope of this latest effort came to vivid life. Paintings always gave the viewer a magnifying glass into life. Whether it was a landscape, a cityscape, mountains, river rapids, meandering cattle, or a freshly bloomed flower.

Art invoked...feelings. A summer's warmth. A winter's chill. Love. Rebirth. Struggle. Strength. Perseverance. Loss.

The oil paintings looking back at her sighed with peace.

She fucking hated them.

That peaceful shit wasn't what she wanted to show the art world. She would rather have burned her newest collection to ashes than allowed her peers to see her name scribbled in the lower right corners.

She hated being known for "life" when her heart was painting death.

Her passion lay in blood and pain and suffering. Her passion had to be kept under lock and key.

Never to be praised by the public.

Art critics would never critique her joy.

She wanted to fit in. She wanted everyday humanity to fulfill *every deep recess of her body. She didn't want to be dark. She didn't want to hide her hate behind a smile.*

She wanted to smile at their faces and stab them in the back when they turned—use their blood to desecrate a fresh white canvas.

No. She hated the pedestrian shit she was about to show the world, but the world wasn't ready to see the real her.

She had been dark for so long. It was getting harder to pretend her smiles were real.

6

———

St Margaret's Hope had never seemed quite as desolate as it did right then. In his fourteen years of living in the secluded village, Finn could not remember it ever being so damned quiet.

Fiona had been moping for the past nine days since their return from Edinburgh and their meeting with Mirren MacGregor. If he were honest—and he really didn't want to be—he'd been moping about too.

Mirren was vibrant. She was wrapped in electric currents that drew him. He wanted to be close to her body even though it would likely burn. He wanted to be the lightning rod to her energy.

The woman drove him mad, but he dreamed of her every night. His dreams were wild, vivid, raw—sexual. More often than not, Finn woke up ferociously pumping his painful erection in his tight fist, imagining Mirren's censorious voice demanding he go faster, harder.

The number of times he had come groaning her name since they'd been home was downright embarrassing. Especially since she clearly couldn't stand him. Before he'd pissed her off, she *had* looked at him with appreciation in her eyes. He hadn't mistaken *that*.

His fantasies had taken over his artist's eye as well, driving him night and day to sketch a collection that featured ambers and golds, diamonds and brown citrine. All shades of that woman's bright-brown eyes and multihued brown waves.

It pissed him off that a snarky girl would give him that burning desire to create. He was surrounded by bits and pieces of crumpled paper showcasing the different expressions of the woman who made them all—Miss Mirren Mòr MacGregor-Morrow.

The burr in his shoe and the reason for his current existence. "I'm manic, for fuck's sake," he groused to himself. Passion and art went hand in hand, and Mirren had certainly sparked a creative livewire in his brain. However, his sister's melancholy was weighing on his conscience.

Fiona didn't complain. It simply wasn't in her nature, but she clearly wasn't above a good guilt trip here and there. They'd argued for three solid days. He had told her to take the opportunity and run with it. She had told him she wouldn't do it without him.

And here she was ghosting round his workshop again. He saw the argument in her eyes before she spoke her first word.

"We both have so much to gain and nothing to lose, Finny," she'd argued. "Don't speak down to me as if I don't know my own brother's talent. You know as well as I do that if those judges saw your work, you'd win, but it seems you've no desire to compete, which I'll have to accept, and that's the end of it."

Except that wasn't the end of it. It was far from the end of it.

"Christ, Fi! How long are you going to sulk over not taking Miss MacGregor up on her offer? You chose to come home, I would remind you." He knew he shouldn't be barking at his sister, but he never could stomach her tears.

"At least I am adult enough to admit I'm scared to live without you. I know you would be okay without me, but you should at least admit you want to move to Edinburgh as much as I do even if it's for different reasons."

That had Finn's dander rising. "First off, lass, I don't want to live without you, but I would if I knew you were safe and it was what you wanted. I'm not fucking selfish, so don't put that on me. Second, I have no reason to want to live in that city ever again." Fiona stiffened at his words. He was on the verge of apologizing and trying to smooth things over when he realized he'd mistaken exasperation for hurt feelings.

Fiona leaned against a workbench in his attached metal shop. Sighing deeply, she crossed her arms and admitted, "I know you always want what's best for me, damn it! You always have. You're the best fucking brother, the best man a person could have standing at their shoulder."

Finn blinked a few times to stop the few tears that were threatening to drop. They never fought, but even during that rare argument, she'd been kind.

Until... "But if you think, Finn Campbell, that I don't know you want to try for that museum competition as badly as I do, you're a nutter. You're also smitten with Mirren. Don't fucking lie to me about that, at least."

He and his sister were facing off with one another, panting in anger and other high emotions, but she was right. "Fuck me," he muttered. She was right on all counts. He wanted to kick every other metal worker's ass, and...Jesus, but he wanted to see that mouthy wee brunette again.

They stood in silence for what felt like hours of self-recrimination and epiphanies, but probably only minutes passed before he finally capitulated. "Let's do it then."

Fiona's head snapped up, and she looked as shell-shocked as he felt. "Wha...wha...what?"

"If you're done berating me, I'll explain."

"Asshole." Finn didn't miss the wobble in her voice or the quick swipe of her eyes with her paint-splattered long-sleeve shirt.

"I do think we're both good enough to have a real shot at winning. I think we're good enough for any competition. It's just that I hate, well, most people, I guess. We've been alone for so long that I'm uncomfortable with crowds."

"Except when you troll the local pubs for a one-nighter," she teased, laughing when his cheeks instantly burned.

Damn his redheaded complexion. "Now who's the asshole?" He did chuckle. There was no use being shy around his best friend. There wasn't a whole lot they didn't know about each other.

"And what about Mirren?"

"What about her?" Finn quickly snapped back. He sighed in defeat at Fiona's raised brow and know-it-all smirk. Sighing, he admitted, "She's an attractive woman. A *very young* attractive woman."

Fiona swiped her hand between them. "Pfft! She's less than ten years younger than you, and you have to admit she's way more mature than most lassies her age. She's also sharp, accomplished, and ambitious. The best part is she calls you on your bad attitude."

Finn leaned against the workbench next to his nosy sister and thought about Mirren. "She tries to goad me." His complaint sounded childish once it left his mouth.

"She does." Fiona laughed. "But what were the odds that she would be the one who owns the *Unkindness*? Does it make you feel better that she has it?"

"Yes. I still want to see it," he replied mulishly, crossing his arms over his chest in irritation.

"Well, you'll surely get your wish since we'll be living with her." She straightened and started toward the door. "Which reminds me, I better go email her before she goes with her second pick."

Finn grasped her arm as she walked by. She looked back. "Fi..." he began, uncomfortable saying what needed to be said. *Did you want to speak to Mirren at lunch?* he didn't add out loud. She knew what he meant.

Her eyes slowly blinked at him for several seconds while the tension in her arm increased. She might have wanted to lie to herself, but she wouldn't lie to him.

"Yes."

"I would never push you, but you've admitted your therapist asked you to find a person that you trust that you would speak to like you do me. Would you consider Mirren a candidate?"

"I want her to be, but...I try to do it. I swear I do. I saw myself so clearly that day in the pub with you and Mirren. I saw myself laughing and talking and teasing, but the words get stuck in my throat. They strangle me.

"The last person I spoke to besides you was...was Dad. I screamed at him to stop. My words, they did nothing, Finn, nothing. My words meant nothing. My screams meant nothing that night. My fucking brain can't seem to find a way around that."

Finn gripped both her slim shoulders, holding her at arm's length so that she could clearly see his face. "Your brain found a way to speak to me, Fi. You did that. You decided to speak to me again, and you damn well did!" He would never let her forget how brave she was.

Having to hear Fiona's remembered pain flayed him wide open. The agony of her having endured that without him—there would never be a day he didn't remember, but he hoped that someday, for both of them, they could fully move past it.

She took several shuddering breaths, her delicate artist's

hands grasping his wrists, anchoring him to her. "I did do that, yes, but you've always and forever been my safe place. From the womb until now. My safe place," she echoed.

"Will you try if we move back to Edinburgh? Can you try?" He needed to hear her say the words.

"I will try. You have my word." Fiona looked away and swallowed deeply. Her nerves were already trying to get the best of her.

He gently shook her shoulders to get her attention again. "Every time you hear that negative voice in your head, you tell it to fuck right off."

She nodded her head in a jerky fashion, but her agreement wasn't given lightly, and Finn knew it.

"We're going to kick ass in this competition." Fiona finally smiled, letting go of his wrists to bop his chin. "Like seriously kick ass."

"I know. Now, get your shit together and email Mouthy Mirren MacGregor."

7

———

Mirren could barely contain the rampant energy ping-ponging from her head to her toes and from her fingers to her middle—a very specific part of her middle. Finn and Fiona Campbell were minutes away from her dad and Josephine's house in Bunchrew.

She had gushed over the twins so much to both sets of her parents that they couldn't wait to meet them. Mirren should have felt guilty about unleashing her family on the Campbells, but they kind of deserved it for torturing her for days after turning down her offer.

T-minus two minutes until plan Mighty MacGregors Overwhelm the Campbells commences.

Mirren was giddy that they'd both agreed to work in Edinburgh. The Smiths were ecstatic to have two talented artists competing for the modern art exhibition and that the Smith Gallery would be their patron for the duration of the competition. At the end of the year, there would be no losers. All eyes would still be on the artists not chosen and the galleries that sponsored them.

Mirren had convinced Kain and Lillias to commit to sponsoring two artists instead of one. However, she was confident that when the twins started producing, the Smiths were going to roll out the red carpet.

Aunt Catriona strolled over and wrapped her strong arm around Mirren's waist. She had at least three inches on her aunt. It had always seemed like Catriona was the tallest in the room, but it was probably due to her giant personality.

"I can't wait for Blair to meet Fiona, Auntie Cat." Mirren bumped her aunt's hip with her own.

"I can't wait either. You seem pretty excited."

Mirren could tell Catriona was fishing. She was only six years Mirren's senior and had always felt more like a big sister.

"I am." She grinned. "They are both incredible artists, and Fiona is one of the sweetest women you'll meet. I'm seriously looking forward to living with her. It'll be nice to have someone else ramble around that giant house Grandma Mary insisted on gifting me."

"Is her brother an asshole?" Catriona asked.

Mirren looked at her aunt sharply. She knew better than to speak about a man who might be in any way connected to Mirren. Her dad and her uncle Coll might overhear, and they were both beasts of burden—specifically, stubborn asses. Her second dad, Charles, was a lot more easygoing on the subject of dating. Her MacGregor dad didn't give a rat's ass that the Campbells were moving in with his daughter for work. His old-fashioned brain kept the phrase "living in sin" on verbal repeat.

Catriona grinned. "I wasn't born last night, Mir. You are way more excited to lay eyes on one of your artists than business demands, but give me some credit," she admonished. "I knew exactly where Thomas, Charles, and Coll were standing. I would rather cut my tongue out than give those overprotective busybodies any reason to snoop into your personal life."

"Sorry." Mirren sighed, properly chagrined. "In my

defense, Dad has been eyeing me for an hour. I realized my mistake when I mentioned Finn's name more than once. At least the little ones are occupying his attention for the moment."

Catriona laughed. "They're trying to settle a dispute between Blair and your sisters. Apparently, wee Margaret decided today was the day she didn't feel like sharing the baby buggy. I caught Mary O'Connor ordering more buggies." Mirren chuckled when Catriona rolled her eyes in the direction of Jo's over-the-top mother.

Margaret was her youngest sister. Mags's terrible twos had nothing on three-year-old Mags. "The moment her daughter married Dad, Mary adopted every single one of us as her own. At least we learned to not bother telling her no. I don't think I've ever seen anyone be successful at trying that."

"So, tell me," Catriona said, veering back to her earlier question, "is Fiona's brother not a good guy? And you should already have expected this, but I heard Coll and Thomas discussing the Campbells' background checks."

"Jesus. Will they ever stop that shit?"

"No. Anyway,"—Catriona brushed off Mirren's irritation—"Thomas didn't like how few details they found. They're both still pissed they only found out two days ago about your new roomies."

That had been purposeful on Mirren's part to avoid exactly what was happening. "They'll dig deeper, then?" Mirren had gotten the impression at lunch that the siblings were alone. Neither had spoken about family, and there was something about Edinburgh that Finn wanted to avoid. Sighing, she admitted, "They are a bit of mystery, but I really dislike prying into their lives."

"Technically, you aren't prying, and there's nothing to do about it. Your dad and Uncle Coll would never let anyone, man or woman, move into your house without finding out if they're a serial killer or something."

"Uncle Coll would hold a parking ticket over their heads." Mirren threw her hands up in surrender.

Catriona laughed. "You're still sore over the hot coals Coll dragged your senior year prom date over."

"I make a point of blocking out anything to do with that incident." In her senior year of high school, Mirren had had friends over, along with the boy she'd liked, Stefen. Coll had grilled him in front of everyone about the plagiarism warning in his school file. *Christ.* Her uncle hacking the school files hadn't even been legal.

"In answer to your question, Finn is not horrible. In his defense—the only one I'll ever give him—I think I rub him the wrong way, which is weird, I know. I'm one of the nicest people I've ever met." Mirren chose to ignore her aunt's snort of amusement.

"Oh, hey, look," Catriona pointed to the outdoor cooking area where everyone was gathered. "Gram must have talked Lyle into coming. How fun. I haven't seen him in ages."

A few years earlier, her uncle Coll and her dad had hired Lyle as extra protection for Gram and Catriona because a crazy drug lord from South America had been after Coll and his family. Gram loved Lyle, so he had become kind of an honorary grandson to her.

Mirren dodged the little girls playing tag around the adults' legs. Their giggling meant the earlier squabble was long forgotten.

"Mir!" Josephine shouted over the racket. "Your friends are here."

Mirren scanned the land around her dad and Josephine's house, and, sure enough, the Campbell twins were making their way over. She'd been thrilled when Fiona had accepted her offer to break their journey from St Margaret's Hope to Edinburgh to enjoy a BBQ with her family.

Mirren hurried to the siblings, shaking hands with the stick-in-the-mud Finn and hugging Fiona. "Before my family cuts off all chances of escape, do either of you need a restroom break?"

Fiona smiled and signed, "I made Finn stop at a petrol station before we got here. I didn't want your family's first impression of me to be the woman waddling to the loo."

"I don't blame you, but if you knew this family, you'd know we would have followed and talked to you through the door." When Fiona signed "OMG," Mirren laughed, partly because the poor woman thought she was teasing.

Finn had yet to speak, but Mirren forgave him when she saw his quick touch to his sister's wrist. They were both nervous and trying to hide it. Well, nothing for it but to throw the two in the deep end of MacGregor.

"I'm so happy you're here. Come meet my family." And she was happy, even about Finicky Finn. Mirren made the rounds quickly so as not to drag out the torture, but when Fiona was introduced to her cousin Blair...oh my, the little girl's eyes rounded in surprise that a stranger was speaking to her in sign.

Fiona, for her part, kept surreptitiously dabbing her eyes at Blair's excitement. When Finn knelt on the ground before the fiery-headed child—Catriona's mini twin—and signed to her that she was wearing a pretty dress, every woman in a five-mile radius had to swallow back tears. Even her uncle Coll looked less like a killer and more like a proud daddy.

Finn Campbell might have had the personality of a hemorrhoid, but when he made Blair huff out a laugh, his shortcomings became a lot less short.

The Campbell intro was going well until Lyle started chatting up Fiona, who was all soft smiles and blushing sighs at the attention. Very aware of how overprotective male minds worked, Mirren could see Finn's outrage building and the unpinned grenades waiting to explode.

When Lyle and Fiona got their cell phones out to communicate, Mirren felt the shift in the air. Finn was a warrior with a cause and about to pull his Viking blade and go on a pillaging rampage. Her dad and uncle were sending looks to one another while keeping the preberserking Campbell in their sights.

The minute Lyle's hand innocently brushed Fiona's shoulder, Finn was mid-sprint before Mirren caught the back of his T-shirt.

"Don't you dare embarrass your sister, Mr. Campbell!" she hissed behind him, not wanting Fiona to be aware of her brother's behavior. "They're exchanging numbers, you oaf. It's what adults do, and last time I checked, at age thirty, Fiona is well into her adulting years."

"I hate being addressed as 'Mr. Campbell,' which I think you are well aware of. Call me by my given name or nothing at all. And if exchanging numbers is so normal, then why don't we have each other's?"

If Mirren were a Victorian miss, she would've stomped her foot and screeched "The nerve!" She wasn't even a smidge Victorian, so she decided on "Because, Finn,"—she put great emphasis on his name—"you are an absolute di—"

"Mirren," her dad growled, Uncle Coll at his shoulder. "Is there a problem here?"

God, no! No, no, no, no. "What? Haha." *Where are your acting skills, Mir? Get your shit together!* "There's no problem. None. Finn and I rib one another all the time. We were just teasing."

"How do you tease each other? You've only met twice to my knowledge." Her dad crossed his arms over his chest, glaring at Finn, who, to his credit, didn't flinch.

So much for keeping the situation under wraps. Fiona, Lyle,

and pretty much everyone else were hanging onto every word of the debacle by then. "Only twice, but as you can see, we are already very comfortable."

"Do you tease each other on the phone?" her uncle Coll asked. *Asshole.*

"Often." Mirren frowned at him, not liking the direction of the conversation.

"It must be difficult to tease over the phone since Finn here just admitted he doesn't have your number."

FML. "I appreciate your concern, Uncle Colly. I'm also starving. Maybe you could concentrate on cooking something." Mirren was about to call in Josephine and her mom for help when Finn shocked her by speaking up.

"I can be too blunt. Too long living in the wilds alone." He shrugged.

On another man, it might have come off as self-deprecating. However, Finn Campbell could never pull off humble.

"Miss MacGregor calls me on my shit. Nothing more." Finn acted disinterested in the whole conversation, but his stiff body language said otherwise.

He glanced sideways for a split second, making eye contact with her. Long enough to ruffle her already ruffled feathers and make her body overwarm. *Prick.*

She would have to remind herself daily that their living arrangement was for one year—only one year. The twins' success would solidify her own. It would be worth it.

Maybe. Probably.

8

Why *am I here?* Finn had asked himself that at least thirty times since they'd arrived at one of Mirren's family addresses. Everyone had been welcoming and kind. It wasn't that. He and Fiona hadn't grown up that way. They didn't have family barbeques or overprotective parents.

He was a fish out of water, gasping for his next unnaturally natural response. Fiona was preoccupied with that dung-eater Lyle, and Finn was left feeling even more egregiously out of place.

Fiona deserved every smile that day was affording her. He'd pushed her to push herself, so he had no right to be angry when she heeded him. He was being childish and reactive and...not himself.

Mirren had been confident during their first meeting, all business professional and charming. Here, amongst her family, she was just as self-assured, only softer. He would never have agreed had someone told him that he lacked that kind of confidence, but the truth was covering his body like a cowardly blanket.

His self-flagellation was interrupted by the sudden appearance of Thomas MacGregor, Mirren's father—one of them anyway—and one intense sonofabitch.

"You're staring at my daughter, Campbell."

"It wasn't intentional," Finn countered. Mirren's step-mother, Josephine, joined them. He really wasn't going to enjoy a moment of silence. It was amusing to watch the unsmiling MacGregor pull Josephine immediately to his side. It was down-right shocking to see him smile softly at his wife after she kissed his cheek.

Josephine smiled and handed Finn a beer. He hadn't real-ized how parched he was until the ice-cold hops slid down his throat. "Thank you, Mrs. MacGregor."

"Jo, please. I've been shopping on your website, Mr. Camp-bell. It is very...ahh, spare."

He snorted at her tact. "Finn, please," he reciprocated. "I hate posting my pieces. I mainly just create what I want and choose different jewelry stores to sell them in."

"Mirren said she's tackling your website soon, so you won't have to worry about that much longer. She's a genius."

"I see." He really did see. Mirren was bossy as hell. She had probably looked at his website, decided it wouldn't do, and put it on her to-do list. MacGregor's raised brows and smirk were grating.

"I bought your raven collection at a shop in Inverness. Mirren fell in love with the tiny gold raven earrings. I bought the collection for her as a surprise. She said you were shocked to see her wearing one of your pieces."

"I was." Finn shrugged, all the while berating himself for appearing aloof. It wasn't his intention to ever be rude. Sighing, he scratched his blunt fingertips through his beard and consid-ered how much longer Fiona would want them to stay.

"You remind me of someone, Finn," Jo started, amusement clear in her tone, "but for the life of me, I can't quite put my finger on who it is." She glanced at her husband and grinned. "Can you, babe?"

It was satisfying to see MacGregor's face turn red. He didn't bother answering his wife. Finn didn't know what the inside joke was, but Jo was clearly teasing her husband.

Not wanting to appear like the dickhead Mirren accused him of being, he said, "Mirren had Fi and me bring most of our completed pieces to catalog. She said it would make a good impression on the museum committee." If he hadn't been so damn desperate to see Mirren again, he would happily be creating more pieces for the competition instead of wading through that unfamiliar, awkward crap.

"It's an exciting opportunity." Josephine smiled and patted him on the arm. Before she wandered off, she thanked him for coming. "We'll be coming for a visit in a few months. Perhaps you can show me some of your metal sculptures. I'd like one for our office."

"I'll look at the space before we leave." Certain pieces belonged in a room, and some didn't.

Finn would have relaxed further against the support beam he was leaning against, but Thomas MacGregor must have had more to say as he was still standing there. Not one to shy away from a conflict, Finn met the man's scowl with one of his own.

"Coll and I ran a background check on you and your sister."

Finn felt every muscle in his body tense and slowly straightened from his slouch. He didn't say anything, unsure whether he could speak without his voice shaking in anger. There had to be something MacGregor wanted to say. Otherwise, he wouldn't have brought it up.

"We own a security company." He shrugged. "It's what we do, and you're to live in her home."

Finn wouldn't argue the precaution. Still...

"You grew up in Edinburgh—no outstanding debt, no

unpaid tickets, no misdemeanors or felonies. Your mother passed when you were a child and your father one year ago. You and your sister were pulled from school at sixteen. School records show you went to live with one of your mother's aunts in the Orkneys."

Finn still didn't respond, but he could feel his face burning in anger.

"You both finished high school and college online. You never went back to Edinburgh. No records of visiting your father. You didn't go to his funeral. Why?"

When Finn had watched true crime documentaries, he'd heard the term "snapped" a thousand times.

It happened to be a very accurate description.

There was no beginning to his actions, only a then. Finn had Thomas MacGregor backed into a corner, his hand around the older man's throat. There was shouting from the guests and the sound of broken glass.

He. Did. Not. Care.

MacGregor didn't fight back. He allowed Finn to hold him in place, which allowed most of the mindless rage to seep from his body. Before he could be pulled off the behemoth threatening his sister, he leaned in and whispered, "I beg you, MacGregor. Don't look any deeper. I promise you that we are safe to be around your daughter, but what you would find in our past would destroy my sister. She would not recover. Please," he begged.

Finn was pulled abruptly from Mirren's father. Coll Barr had him in a chokehold. Finn was trying to decide whether to fight or surrender when Mirren's face came into focus—her furious face.

"You better have a good fucking reason for holding Finn, Uncle Coll, or I can assure you, all hell is about to break loose. On your face!"

"Mir—"

"Don't you 'Mir' me, Colly." The brunette bombshell whipped her head to MacGregor, her face red and splotchy. "Explain this, Dad. Please explain this," she sniffled.

Thomas MacGregor had less armor against the lass than Finn and caved the minute he saw his daughter's distress—but not in the way Finn would have imagined.

"I'm all in for the Glasgow Warriors, and this wet-behind-the-ears pup is an Edinburgh Rugby fan. It's blasphemous, Mir. Surely, you can see that."

MacGregor was laying it on thick, and if Mirren's narrowed eyes shouted anything, it was that she didn't believe a word out of her father's mouth. As Coll let Finn go, Fiona was there throwing her arms about his chest and basically making him feel about as unmanly as a man could feel, but he clasped her tight regardless, knowing she needed the comfort more than he needed his pride.

Finn looked at MacGregor over Fiona's shoulder and gave a brief nod of thanks. He hoped the man would back off and leave the past where it was. Buried.

Josephine was there touching her husband's cheek briefly. The man kissed his wife's palm and said loudly, "Let's get the steaks on before Campbell tries to convert my daughters over to the losing team." He shook his head. "Christ...Edinburgh."

The moment passed—oddly—but at least the tension was cut off. He would thank MacGregor if there was a moment for it. MacGregor's oldest daughter was clearly not appeased. She looked at him with a multitude of emotions; the foremost was concern, and that gutted him.

"Rugby?"

Finn shrugged but didn't elaborate.

Mirren sighed, glancing at Fiona and Lyle, who were a short

distance away. "Are you alright? Would you like to leave now? I'll leave too," she added quietly.

He felt his heart pounding fiercely at her thoughtful question. She was putting his feelings above her family...above her own. He would never forget that moment.

He wanted to take Mirren in his arms and kiss her until they couldn't breathe. He wanted to do...a lot of things, but he knew that barbeque was something Mirren had looked forward to, according to Fi, and he wouldn't ruin her day.

"I would like to stay."

She cocked her head, probably contemplating his honesty, before saying, "Okay, Finn." His knees almost buckled when he felt one of her fingers lightly drag across the top of his left hand as she passed him.

9

———

The barbecue was over. Josephine had taken Fiona and Finn inside to show them the office she and her dad shared. Jo had mentioned earlier that she'd told Finn she was interested in purchasing one of his sculptures.

That had left Mirren in a stare-down with her dad standing by the cars. She'd already said her goodbyes to everyone, and no one had followed them to the driveway. They could probably tell she needed a minute or two of private time with the most over-the-top father in the world.

"What happened, Dad? Really. I know it had nothing to do with rugby. I saw you and Finn shake hands later, so he must not have done anything too unforgivable." Seeing her father and Finn locked in a heated...something...had shaken her. Finn had looked ferocious and vulnerable simultaneously.

Mirren had been sure that the men were about to come to blows. Her body was still shaking two hours later. She hated not knowing why they'd argued, but she wasn't a nosy teenager any longer. She was still nosy, only old enough to bide her time.

That time had arrived.

Her dad breathed out a breath that sounded an awful lot

53

like surrender. Mirren's brows winged up. She'd expected a fight or a bit of push and pull, at least. Her dad didn't lie. He may have omitted, but Thomas MacGregor had too much integrity for lies.

"I touched a nerve with Campbell when I mentioned MacGregor Security had been working on a background check on him and his sister."

"What?" Mirren's sharp tone made her dad wince. "Why would you tell him? You only do that if you've found some—" Mirren cut off the thought. A crushing feeling swamped her chest. "You found something?"

"No. Coll and I found nothing."

Confused, she asked, "And that's a bad thing?"

"Things got heated when I said I would continue to look into them." He scrubbed a hand over his face and shook his head. "I underestimated him. I rarely do that. The only thing I will tell you, Mir, is that I believe the siblings are good people, and most of my unease was relieved after meeting them today.

"They *are* hiding something. If I had to guess, it's something from their childhood before they moved from Edinburgh. I won't lie to you. I will find out, and before you berate me, you know Uncle Coll wouldn't allow me a minute's rest if I didn't. But"—he paused to give her a stern look—"unless the news would affect you in some way, I won't tell you what I find. The Campbells can tell you or not.

"He only got angry today in defense of his sister. He was honoring his family, and I won't dishonor either of them by sharing a tale that isn't mine." Her dad pulled her into a hug and patted her back, which he still didn't understand felt as nurturing as the Heimlich. "Are we good?"

"Of course, Dad." Mirren attempted to hide her wheeze as he pounded out the last of her lungs' oxygen.

"I'm proud of you and what you're doing for the Smiths."

"Of course you are," Mirren teased. "What parent wouldn't be?"

Ignoring her sass, he asked, "You'll call me if you need me?"

He asked that same thing every time she visited. "Always." She hated that she had to swallow back tears. She loved her life in Edinburgh, but she loved her family more. It was hard not to see them every day.

Mirren heard the crunching of gravel behind her and could feel Finn's intense gaze without turning around. Her dad let her go but kept her close to his side.

He offered his hand to Fiona first before signing a quick, "You are welcome any time."

Mirren could tell Fiona was touched if her glassy eyes were any indication. He shook Finn's hand next.

"I'm trusting you, Campbell, with one of my most precious gifts. You will protect her as you do your own sister." It wasn't a request.

Finn must have spoken her dad's language. He nodded his assent and shook hands before he led his sister to their waiting truck and enclosed trailer.

Jo gave Mirren a big hug. "I love you, Mir. Call me when you get home."

"I love you too, Jo. You realize Dad and Uncle Colly will be tracking me every minute?" Mirren had learned years ago that telling the men in her family to back off was like asking the sun not to rise and set.

"Oh, I know." While her dad watched them both with a fond smile, Jo leaned close and whispered where he couldn't hear. "I know you're lusting after Finn. I wanted you to know that I approve. You just have to promise to keep me updated." And before Mirren choked on her own tongue, Jo added, "I'm pregnant with your baby brother. Your dad and I wanted you to be the first to know. Don't you dare tell my mom yet."

Mirren sucked in a surprised breath so fast she choked, throwing her arms around the best stepmother in the world. "Oh, wow," Mirren choked out, tears dripping from her eyes, "I'm so happy for you." Mirren grabbed her dad's hand and dragged him close, making him bend so she could kiss his cheek. "Congratulations, Dad. You finally get a son!" Mirren laughed and squeezed his hand in hers.

"Never think another daughter would have made me any less happy, lass. My girls are everything to me." When tears threatened his own eyes, he gruffly told her to get on the road. "I don't want you driving after dark."

As Mirren was sliding into her sleek black BMW Coupé, she made eye contact with Finn through the front windshield of his Toyota pickup.

He signed a question. "You're upset?"

Mirren signed back, "Happy tears," and then, "Try to keep up, old man." She laughed as he shook his head in exasperation. The next few months were about to be very interesting.

10

F inn looked around his new workspace with satisfaction. Mirren had given him permission to take over the gardening cottage. It sat just behind the house, only a few feet from the home's mudroom. It was brilliant to be able to throw his dirty clothes in the laundry and shower before ever entering the main living area. He'd chosen the small bedroom nearest to the mudroom for even more efficiency.

It didn't hurt that his room was closest to the kitchen. Working with metal, especially his sculptures, burned a lot of calories.

It had taken him a while to come up with a layout for the cottage and all of his tools, but he was definitely satisfied with the result. A long wooden potting table had been converted into his jewelry design station. The bank of windows above provided perfect lighting.

He'd brought most of his metal sculpting equipment to Edinburgh—metal files and rasps, a welder, a hammer and an anvil, and an angle grinder. It had been worth the inconvenience of moving his shop here. He would be working on at least two sculptures for the Smith Gallery exhibit that he knew

*—he knew—*had real chances of winning him a place in the Scottish National Gallery of Modern Art.

He wanted to win. He wanted his sister to win too. They did everything together, and he didn't want to experience that without her.

He and Fiona agreed that neither of them had felt so inspired in the studio in years. The last time he'd felt that free was when he was a fifteen-year-old teenager dreaming of the *Unkindness.*

Once their father had hurt Fiona, he'd felt like a part of his creative mind, the part that relied on innocence or wonder or hope, had been buried.

It was a relief that they hadn't lost the sense of adventure that they'd found in creating as children. In their own ways, the siblings had put parts of themselves away, like adults tucking their childhood treasures into boxes to shove in the backs of closets. Forgotten.

Finn leaned back in his chair and slowly spun. At least forty sketches were hanging all topsy-turvy from the walls, and more were scattered over tabletops and chairs. He could look at them for hours while his mind conjured the steps he would take to bring them to life. It was like having his own library of short films.

They'd been living in Edinburgh for two months, and he finally felt like he was getting used to living in the city again. The first couple of weeks had been nothing but unpacking. His had taken a lot longer than Fiona's, of course.

He rarely saw Mirren but felt her presence everywhere on the property, especially in his bed at night—because he brought her there. Finn's grand imagination wasn't limited to jewelry.

If their paths did cross, it was her sprinting to her car to meet artists, potential new artists, or clients who wanted Mirren to travel to their homes and recommend pieces for them.

Normally, Finn would have scoffed at someone who wasn't an artist recommending art. Still, he admitted that Mirren was gifted in that area.

He'd once thought that Mirren was an overpaid layabout. Living with her for two months had disabused him of the ignorant notion. There were days, though, when it felt like she was avoiding him. Why would she do that? He was sure they'd moved past his poor first impression.

They'd had a moment at her parents' barbecue. He was sure of it.

She never avoided his sister.

He frowned as he locked up the cottage and made his way to the mudroom. It was irritating that she might be dodging him. It was doubly annoying that it was bothering him so much. He would normally ask himself whether he'd unintentionally offended her since moving in, but as their interactions were rare and short, he didn't think so. Fiona would have told him if he'd screwed up.

Mirren would have to see him tonight, though, since she had a rare early night and she and Fiona were cooking an Italian feast for the three of them. He would need to shower quickly. Doctoring the French baguettes was his job, and he was running behind.

He pushed open the back door to the mudroom, already pulling his dirty T-shirt over his head, and froze. Mirren was standing by the farmhouse sink, a dress in one hand and a bottle of stain remover in the other. The dress must have come off her body because a bra and panties were the only things she was wearing.

Her mouth rounded in a comic O, her eyes widened, and her arms froze in midair. The bra and matching panties were sheer and silky and a deep wine color and did nothing to disguise the perfection of the woman's figure. He allowed himself the briefest of glances—he was only human, and Mirren MacGregor was pure fantasy—before spinning on his heel and raising his hands in...surrender? Definitely surrender.

Her stammered "K...k...kill me" reached his ears and made his lips twitch in amusement.

"Forgive me, lass. Was this invitation for dinner *and* a show?" he asked over his shoulder. Finn expected growling, but he got a surprising burst of laughter instead.

"Oh my God," Mirren snickered. "I'm sorry, Finn. Truly. I'm beyond embarrassed. Fiona and I were cooking, and I opened up a can of stewed tomatoes and splattered the front of my dress. It's one of my favorite dresses!"

He felt like he was acting out the first thirty seconds of one of his sister's favorite rom-coms. The least he could do was not embarrass himself by flirting.

"Dark red is one of my favorite colors. Did you know that, or were your skivvies an ode to Italian night?" So he wasn't above flirting...with his much younger housemate. Not that it was good flirting. He had no game.

"Haha, asshole." Mirren was quick with her comeback. "Fi warned me that you could be a trial to live with. I admit"—she paused, probably for impact—"I wasn't surprised."

"My sister has a big mouth." He heard rustling, which meant she was probably putting on a new outfit. Mirren never did the expected. Her amusement at him catching her undressed was...irritating. Had he wanted her breathless? Overwhelmed with lust at the sight of his bare chest?

"So, you like red, Mr. Campbell?"

Finn jumped, barely stifling an unmanly squeak of surprise. Unbeknownst to him, Mirren had come up close behind him, whispering her words close enough to his naked back to make him shiver. "I do," was all he could manage.

Silence stretched between them. He wanted nothing more

than to swing around and confront the saucy woman invading his space.

"Best hurry, Campbell. Garlic bread waits for no man."

Finn didn't move for a full minute after Mirren walked away. His body was on fire, and telling it that the object of his fascination hadn't touched his back for any reason other than casual contact wasn't easing the heat.

He hadn't imagined Mirren tracing his lower spine. No way. She'd touched him, and it hadn't felt casual.

FIONA COULDN'T TAKE one bite of her spaghetti without picking her phone up. It was annoying as all hell. So were Mirren's sighs and soft smiles. They knew something that he didn't know, and his already short fuse was shorter thanks to seeing Miss MacGregor in her underthings—her distractingly sexy underthings.

"Am I missing something?" he asked aloud without bothering to sign since his sister could hear him just fine even though her face was an inch from her phone screen. Her slight frown proved that she'd heard his question.

"Oh, leave her alone, Finn," Mirren admonished. "Lyle is a stand-up guy. Dad and Uncle Coll wouldn't have hired him to run a MacGregor Security team if he wasn't. Plus, you and I can live vicariously through your sister since neither of us has a social life. Though, at least I landed a date tomorrow."

Finn felt his skin prickle with anger. Entirely unfair, but he didn't give a shit. "Do you, now?" Fiona glanced up at his tone. Mirren was too busy twisting noodles about her fork to notice his agitation. Or was she purposely avoiding looking at him? There was a tenseness to her shoulders that he'd never seen.

Sighing, she looked at him with a wide smile. Almost too

wide. "Yeah. Lance is a reporter for the Daily Mail. He has done several great articles on Scottish artists over the years. I'm looking forward to hearing all the Daily Mail gossip about the artistic world."

Swallowing the growls that were trying to escape, Finn smiled good-naturedly and said, "I'm sure you have your favorite restaurants, but I suggest you try Golden Pizzeria & Cocktails. It's been years since I've been there, but you haven't had pizza until you've tried theirs."

Mirren's eyes sparkled as she met his gaze, absently licking a drop of spaghetti sauce from the edge of her full bottom lip. A flash of him leaning forward to lick it off himself before sweeping his tongue into her mouth had Finn exhaling a deep breath in an attempt to diffuse his lust-addled brain. *Christ, save me.*

"Oh! I've wanted to go there for months, but they have such a waiting list, or the lines are so long, I just give up."

"I know the owners. Allow me to get you a table." Mirren suddenly looked uneasy. They *had* just semiflirted in the laundry while they were both partially undressed, and at that moment, he was happily helping her with her dinner date.

She should have been suspicious. He was desperate to know whether she had thought about their half-dressed chance encounter. Did she like his body as much as he liked hers?

What Mirren didn't know was how difficult the past weeks had been. Pretending he didn't have feelings besides cordiality was taxing. He and Mirren hadn't shared more than a handshake. He wanted more.

They were living together, and his eight-year-old self had called dibs. He wasn't prepared to see her dating.

Thomas MacGregor had entrusted Finn with Mirren's safety. That Lance could have been fine, or he could have been a piece of shit or a serial killer. Finn would be remiss if he didn't discover which one he was. He owed it to MacGregor.

Mirren let her fork slip from her fingers and clank the side of the ridiculously expensive china they were using. "That's very kind of you, Finn. Thank you."

Feeling lighter than he had in days, he just shrugged and smiled. Fiona finally put her phone aside and gave him a questioning glare. He ignored her like the irritating brother he was.

"Leave it to me. I'll let you know what they have available so you can let Leslie know."

Narrowing her eyes, Mirren corrected, "Lance."

"Of course."

11

Competitors.

    Competition.

Fuck that.

If she could show her real work, no one could stand against her.

She inhaled a deep gulp of air. She could feel herself spiraling. Vitriol was slowly replacing the blood in her veins.

She slammed her fist on the bleached wood of the old table pressed against her hips. "You aren't good enough, you dumb cow!" She ignored the spittle that had flown from her mouth and landed on the freshly painted scape laid in front of her.

"Oh, now you're going to cry," she sneered. "It isn't my fault you're shit. Look at you! You're a disgusting mess."

Banging both fists against the table's surface rattled the jars of linseed oil and paint thinner, causing a few brushes to spill out and stain the rough wood. She spun on her heel and began pacing the sunny attic.

"There must be a way," she whispered to herself. "This pathetic excuse for a collection will never get me that spot in the Scottish National Gallery of Modern Art."

She could barely think because of the annoying, pathetic sniffles coming from an equally annoying, pathetic woman. She went to the bank of windows that overlooked the front garden and sighed as she saw her brother making his way to the house.

"Damn it," she growled, exasperated at being interrupted. After patting her cheeks and touching up her hair, she looked at the collection once more as she made her way out of the room.

"Pathetic. Absolutely pathetic," she tsked. "Fix this shit or you'll never leave this room."

12

____

The Golden Pizzeria & Cocktails lived up to its name and more. The décor was luxurious, and the bar's selection was crazy. Finn must have known the owners well because she and Lance had been treated to a chef's table and endless appetizers and cocktails.

Lance was fine company...kind of. Truth? He was terrible. She kept wishing that she were enjoying the evening with the Campbells—one particular Campbell. The one with a god's physique.

A shirtless Finn had left Mirren restless for hours the night before. No man should be that sigh-worthy. Had she known what the man was hiding under his shirt, she would have contrived a way to ogle him sooner.

He had definitely flirted with her, and he had definitely checked out her body before facing away. For those two reasons, Mirren couldn't help but flirt back. Avoiding Finn Campbell had become increasingly difficult because she lived to catch even a glimpse of the man. After the previous night, the prospect held no appeal.

And if she were honest, she'd never been good at not going

after what she wanted. School, work, making deals... She always ended up on top. She wanted to be on top of Finn. Shaking her head slightly to knock off the sexual thoughts, she attempted to bring her focus back to her date.

Golden's owners came by to introduce themselves. Alex and Sadie Gold were as gregarious as an Italian-American pairing could be. They gushed over Finn but never actually said how they knew him or when they had first met.

Lance wasn't amused at hearing accolades bestowed on another man. *Inferiority complex much?*

An hour into the evening, Sadie dropped by to deliver a bottle of wine that "Mr. Campbell had picked out especially for Miss MacGregor and Leslie." She felt more than she saw her date stiffen. Whether it was because another man was buying his date a bottle of expensive wine or because his name had been botched, he was clearly incensed. Sighing, Mirren stiffened her backbone and prepared for an extraordinarily long night.

The evening's faux pas didn't stop there. Mrs. Gold went on to gush, saying, "Finn and his sister surprised us by stopping by tonight," and "I haven't seen them for years. Had I known they were in town, I would have shut the whole place down for a private evening, but Alex and I are so thrilled to see them."

What a coincidence...

Why would Finn offer to get her and her date a reservation and then come himself...at the same time? Surely, it didn't mean... No. No, no, no. Mirren wouldn't get her hopes up.

When she'd mentioned having a date, she would have sworn Finn hadn't been thrilled, but would he try to sabotage it? Whatever his motivation, she didn't want to spend the evening questioning Finn Campbell's motives.

So, of course, she did nothing but question them. *Damn*

him. If he was interested in her as a woman, then why didn't he make a move? They lived together, for the love of God.

Only mind-altering voodoo could have erased the thrill of them flirting with each other in the laundry. He had looked at her like she was a desirable woman, and she had...touched him. Christ, but his body was built from the hard labor of his craft. The night before, her dreams had featured every cut and hollow of his chest and back that she'd seen and created an image about the parts she hadn't.

Mirren glanced at Lance, deciding not to feel guilty about fantasizing about another man. Lance was nice enough, but he was a stranger and one who enjoyed talking about himself.

He was classically handsome. Light-brown hair cut and styled perfectly, blue eyes, a square jaw, a fitted suit that showed off his lean body—he was an avid runner, which she knew because he'd spent fifteen minutes detailing his hobbies—and faultless table manners.

Once Lance ran out of Lance stories, the interrogation about the Smiths' chosen competitors for the museum exhibit began. Her irritation and unease rose with each question.

Her daddy hadn't raised a fool. She might have been late to catch on, but it was clear that either Lance had wanted to date her and was using it as an opportunity to pump her for inside information about the Smiths, or his only interest in Mirren was what she might add to a Daily Mail article.

She was leaning toward the latter.

"Tell me, Mirren, is Smith Gallery going to sponsor an artist to compete in the Scottish National Gallery competition?"

"As I'm sure you're aware, Lance, most galleries, private sponsors, and even the artists prefer to stay anonymous as long as possible. There are still patrons who would try to poach rival gallery artists and even spiteful artists that might go as far as sabotage." That level of malice happened rarely, but it did happen.

"I'm aware." Lance's increasingly grating voice had turned condescending. "There is chatter all over the country, however, which means it's only a matter of time before all the names are dropped. Surely"—Lance leaned across the table with what he probably thought was a sigh-worthy grin—"you would give me the tiniest lead."

"I won't, no." The quickly covered anger that flashed over his face proved that the evening had purely been a fact-digging expedition. At least her instincts were online.

"Rarely is my intuition off. You disappoint me."

"I'm sure you'll survive. Let's split the bill and call it a night, shall we?" Mirren caught their waiter's attention and got the bill. She quickly calculated her half plus a generous tip and paid in cash. Lance did the same.

She couldn't remember ever meeting a slimier human. Her family would have disliked him immensely. Her uncle Coll would have wanted to ruin him. Mirren wanted only to stick a fork in his hand.

When Lance stood, Mirren followed suit. Before she could thank him for dinner, Lance struck again. "Perhaps we should go and find our benefactor and thank them personally for the wine."

Whether due to his reporter's hunch or just bad luck, declining would have raised his suspicious nature. He didn't know the Campbells were the very artists he had been asking after earlier. She just had to play it cool and somehow warn them not to mention their profession.

Mirren responded, "That's a grand idea."

As she and Lance made their way to the polished bar in the center of the restaurant that rivaled many art installations, Mirren sucked in a breath as her eyes met Finn's. Lance took that moment to place his hand on her lower back, asserting an unwanted possessiveness after their uncomfortable evening. If Finn's frown was an indicator, he didn't like the man touching her either.

Thinking fast, Mirren smiled up at Lance to put him at ease before quickly signing to the Campbells, "I'll explain later. Don't admit you are artists. This guy is a snake. Behave, Finn, or you will pay later."

The bar was full to capacity, so she and Lance stood behind Finn and Fiona, who spun their barstools around to accommodate conversation. She signed the exchange so Lance would understand that Fiona was deaf.

"Finn, Fiona! This is Lance Merte. I wanted to introduce everyone, and we both wanted to thank you, Finn, for the lovely bottle of wine. Lance," she dipped her head to the prick at her shoulder, "these are my good friends, Finn and Fiona Campbell. They are old family friends and own a highly successful house flipping business in Inverness."

Everyone shook hands, but Finn clearly didn't understand the "behave" memo. He never smiled, and Mirren was positive she saw Lance wince when they shook.

"Lance," Finn practically spit the name. "Mirren and I live together. How nice to meet one of her young friends."

Oh, the insult...

Fiona quickly signed, and Mirren translated. "Fiona said that they are living with me for a few months while they look at several properties here in Edinburgh."

"They are considering opening a second location here. It's very exciting."

At least Lance tried for cordiality—more than he'd shown her at the end of their date anyway—replying, "You must be flooded with homes to flip here. There seems to be no end of dilapidated properties in Edinburgh. My mother is in real estate. Have Mirren call me if you two are interested in her showing you some listings."

Finn signed, "Tell him to fuck off and go home."

"Sorry, Lance, sometimes Finn forgets to speak out loud for the hearing. He asked what you do for a living." It was a safe gambit. Lance did love to speak about himself.

"I'm a journalist. I write for the Daily Mail." He sniffed in self-importance, lifting his chin, attempting and failing to show his superiority.

Could the wiener have preened any harder? How in the world had she ever accepted a date offer from the dingleberry? That was one of Josephine's favorite slurs from her home state of Oklahoma, where she'd grown up. Mirren had always loved it.

In a feat of wizardry, Finn signed, "Make better choices, lass, or you're never leaving the house again," while asking Lance, "What do you mainly write about, Lance?" as if he were interested.

"I'm known for my interest in the art world. Galleries and artists ask me to cover their exhibits. I'm highly sought after."

Even Fiona blinked at the man's shameless bragging.

Somehow, Finn kept a straight face when he said, "Ahh, you and Mirren must have had no end of conversation starters for your first date since your passions run the same path."

"I had hoped," was all Lance the Lame answered.

Fiona simply nodded her head. Finn gritted his teeth but kept his slightly interested mien in place. Mirren didn't even think her dad could have kept his cool that long.

"Lance, it was a pleasure to meet you." Finn stood to shake the other man's hand again and probably show off the difference in their builds to better advantage. Finn was taller, broader, and —in Mirren's opinion—way more handsome. Finn continued, "If you two are calling it a night, I would be more than happy to see Mirren safely home. It's no trouble. As I mentioned, my sister and I are currently living with her."

Ahh... Finn was making sure Lance knew Fiona was his sister and not his girlfriend. Read: "I'm single and ready to mingle." *Save me from alpha males, Lord Jesus.*

"How convenient. Of course," Lance gritted. "Thank you again for the wine, Mr. Campbell." Glancing at Fiona, he said a perfunctory "Ms. Campbell" and then said to his date, "Mirren. Goodnight."

13

"Thanks again for setting up tonight's reservation. That place was fantastic, and Alex and Sadie were so kind. They never said how they know you."

Finn straightened a coffee mug on one of the kitchen shelves, ignoring the question. He had no wish to discuss his teenage years. Not that night. Thankfully, Mirren didn't pry.

"Such a shame my date only asked me out to pump me for information about you and your sister."

Speaking of sisters, Fiona had run off to her room the second they'd gotten home. He really needed to speak to Mirren's father about Lyle. Finn understood that if the man worked for MacGregor Security, then they had to have trusted him, but as he was the first man Fiona had ever shown an interest in, he needed more than Lyle having a fine work CV.

Fiona could see whomever she chose. It was just different... weird. It had been the two of them for so long. He was embarrassed to even admit to himself that he felt left out or left behind somehow.

Mirren had offered to make some tea before heading to bed. Finn had accepted. Of course, he'd accepted. He'd seen more of

Mirren in the last few days than in the last few weeks combined. He wasn't ready for it to end.

He was also curious about her date. "Why did you have Fi and me lie about our work? Not that I minded. It's weasels like him that make me glad I don't live in a big city anymore."

"You do live in a big city," she reminded him.

"Temporarily," he shot back, and just to keep her on her toes, he added, "You looked lovely tonight." Her breathy "oh" made him smile. She wouldn't know since her back was turned to him while she fiddled with the kettle.

She was wearing a dark-amber silk button-up with loose blue jeans and red heels. When he'd seen her walking toward him with her "date," sweat had broken out across his brow. Mirren MacGregor was stunning.

"Leslie is a moron if he didn't tell you."

She slowly turned and looked at him with raised brows. "Lance," she emphasized the correct name, "isn't blind. He's just a prick. I know I look good," she added while pretending to fluff her hair, as if she had a vain bone in her body. Mirren was proof that a person could own confidence without wearing a narcissistic cloak.

"I asked you to lie because he was trying to wheedle information about whether or not Smith Gallery was sponsoring any artists for the exhibit competition.

"He let slip that his sister is an artist. Hannah works in oil like Fiona. Before I accepted a dinner date with Lance, I didn't realize they were related. I've seen some of her work. She's very talented but extremely unkind and full of herself."

"Those two apples clearly fell from the same tree." Finn shook his head in wonder at how some people lived to cut others down.

"Exactly. I got the impression that Lance is helping his sister uncover who her competition is. It's gross and completely unprofessional."

"Why would they want to know? I don't get it." Finn was truly confused. "You'd think they would rather know who the judges will be so they can chat them up."

Finn hadn't known Mirren long, but he did believe, without a doubt, that she was an honest person—sometimes too honest. So when she glanced to the side in discomfort at his question, Finn got a queer sense of foreboding in his belly.

"What's going on, Mir?"

She quickly looked at him. It was the first time he'd used her nickname. She leaned her back against the countertop and sipped her tea, probably contemplating what to tell him.

He took a step closer, keeping only a couple of feet between them. "What don't you want to tell me?"

"Listen, I'm still mulling this evening over. I didn't want to raise my concerns if they proved unfounded. I wanted to speak with Dad too. However, if someone like Lance is rooting around, it might be because they hope to dig up information to tarnish or discredit a person.

"There are a few journalists who have dug up dirty laundry on gallery owners and collectors and published it this past year. Most of us despise the practice, but it doesn't negate the fact that the story is out there. To my knowledge, Lance hasn't written any articles like that. It would cost him in the art world, but it doesn't mean he wouldn't chance it for the fame."

Finn didn't respond. He waited, hoping she would decide to tell him why she was worried where he and Fiona were concerned.

"I've told you already that I quickly realized Lance was using the date as a way to gather information on possible artists entering the competition. I'm sure I wasn't the first person to meet him under false pretenses, nor will I be the last. He is known as an excellent art reporter, but before I accepted the date with him, I did do a light background check on him."

Finn hadn't liked Thomas MacGregor doing a background check on him, but he couldn't help but smile. "Talk about two other apples that fell from the same tree."

She grinned at the comparison, looking rather pleased with herself. "Anyway, I found that Lance has recently been trying his hand at investigative reporting. He's written a few articles about political candidates and one about a primary school closing due to a lack of funding.

"Not dirty laundry reporting, but I believe it was his new investigative skills he tried to use on me tonight. He bored me with his tedious stories while slipping in questions about Smith." Her smile withered.

Finn felt himself stiffen at the word "investigative" He set his tea aside. Mirren followed suit. He watched as she reached for his hand, almost like she was about to reassure him with her touch. He was disappointed when her arm fell back to her side.

He could have used some reassurance.

Mirren swiped her hand between them. "Let me backtrack to my family's cookout. The one you and Fiona went to," she clarified unnecessarily.

She was nervous; her clasped hands at her waist gave that emotion away. He scanned the hallways leading into the kitchen, making sure Fiona wasn't on her way back.

"You and Dad had a disagreement. I asked him about it before we left." Finn must have looked alarmed because she took his hand then. "Dad said he mentioned the background check and it pissed you off when he said he was going to keep digging."

Finn remained silent, afraid his voice might shake and give him away. He dropped his gaze to focus on her hands, enfolding one of his much larger ones. Her thumbs were hypnotizing as they made circles over the back.

"I will tell you that he thought you and Fiona were good people, but because you were going to be living with his daughter, nothing would stop him from knowing if your past could affect me. At the same time, he very clearly stated that he would never reveal what he found. Not to his wife. Not to me. Certainly not to anyone else.

"He respects that you love your sister. He respects you, Finn, which is a big deal for him.

"It's because I knew he thought you were hiding something that Lance's queries, combined with his job, made me uneasy. I was honest when I reminded him that most patrons and artists prefer anonymity. Though there are always those who are vocal as well.

"If you have a past that you'd prefer to keep secret, and knowing that you also once lived in Edinburgh, I suggest you keep the competition quiet. I plan on making sure Kain and Lillias keep your names to themselves. I'm sure the ask is unnecessary. The Smiths are beyond professional. They will assuredly ignore all queries about the competition."

Finn took several minutes to digest Mirren's revelations. His greatest fear of the last fourteen years felt like it was wrapping a noose around his neck. He could tell Fiona what might be waiting for them and pull them both from the competition, run back to their lonesome life in St Margaret's Hope, and continue to live as they had before moving. Or they could lie low in Edinburgh and hope their past didn't catch up with them.

Fiona had been a different person since they'd moved there. She smiled often. She loved Mirren like a sister, and Lyle... She obviously cared for that slick sonofabitch.

He'd been slowly coming to the conclusion that living as they had been had allowed Fiona to stay in a bubble. One that hadn't required stepping outside her comfort zone. He'd been complacent enough to stay in the bubble with her.

He was disappointed that she hadn't opened up to Mirren more. She had promised him that she would work toward speaking to people other than him. She believed that admitting to a stranger that she had issues with selective mutism would mean that she would have to explain what trauma had caused it.

She never had to tell anyone. Ever. There were good people out there, like Mirren, who wouldn't expect or require an explanation. Finn had even considered outing his sister and telling Mirren himself the other night but had discarded the idea almost immediately. He wouldn't add his betrayal to Fiona's traumas.

All those years later, the ghost of what their dad had done still haunted them. Finn hadn't saved her. He'd been too late, and Fiona had suffered because of it.

Mirren let go of his hand and hopped up on the kitchen counter and sat, letting her legs dangle in the air. "Can you tell me what you're thinking, Finn? Would it help to talk it through with me, or maybe you should speak to your sister and see what she thinks?"

There were a lot of things he should have been doing, and talking to his sister was high on the list, but he found himself stepping in front of Mirren instead. Her slightly spread knees were an invitation he chose to prioritize.

14

Mirren watched Finn advance but kept silent. He was satisfied, though, when her legs spread just that little bit wider. Finn moved slowly. He wanted no misunderstanding about his intention to touch her and no misunderstanding that he had her permission. That she wanted him to.

The first touch of his palms against her jean-clad knees had them both sucking in air. He knew he'd wanted Mirren MacGregor from the moment he'd watched her smile across the Smith Gallery at his sister.

She had been so lovely and so genuine—and then he'd seen his raven at her throat. It had felt like a sign. He hadn't wanted to sell the collection, but he had.

And it had ended up in her hands.

He let his fingers curl around the slender tops of her legs, letting his thumbs drag and put pressure against the pants' side seam. He widened her legs enough to step fully in the breach and leaned down.

"Did you like seeing me without a shirt on yesterday?"

There was no hesitation when she answered. "Yes."

"Did you want to do anything else to me besides touch my back?"

She leaned closer to him that time so that her breath was fanning his lips. He couldn't stop from groaning. He kept his hands sliding ever higher.

She softly admitted, "A lot more."

"I couldn't sleep from remembering how that red silk looked against your skin. I could see your nipples were puckered and the outline of your slit. Christ, Mir, I wanted to come to your room that night." He hesitated before adding, "I've wanted to come to your room every night since I've lived here."

"Why didn't you, then?"

"Several reasons. I'm your guest. I didn't know how you felt about me. I'm too old for you. And the most deadly serious reason, your dad probably injected me with a tracker during that cookout so he would know if I entered his precious daughter's bedroom."

Mirren huffed a laugh. The barest touch of their lips had his body hardening uncomfortably against his zipper.

She placed her hands on his shoulders, fingers brushing his neck. "You are my guest, but I don't believe either of us agreed to a no touching rule. You didn't know how I felt about you because I was too afraid to put myself out there in case you shot me down."

She held three fingers up. "Maybe you should consider doing a background check on my family and friends. I think you'll find that age has never been an issue with us. As for the last...the tracker...I wouldn't put it past him. I'm willing to chance it if you are."

He couldn't decide whether she was joking about that last bit or not, and he lost interest in figuring it out when her mouth suddenly fused to his. His focus became her taste and how the slide of her tongue felt against his.

He held on to her back and pulled her body flush to his. She wrapped her legs around his waist and held his face between her hands to pull his mouth exactly where she wanted.

"God, I love your beard, Finn," she said while scratching her fingers against his cheeks, jawline, and neck.

"I know you said red is your favorite color, but from the minute you walked into Smith, I've been obsessed with the color too. I've lost hours of sleep over you, Finn Campbell."

Her admission made his chest tighten in pleasure. He broke the kiss so he could rip his T-shirt over his head, needing to feel Mirren's hands on his bare skin. He groaned in pleasure the minute her palms skated over his chest and around his back. Her blunt tiny nails pressed into his skin.

"Christ, I love you touching me." He skimmed over the buttons of her blouse. "Can I?" Without breaking the kiss, she moaned and nodded her assent. He'd never unbuttoned a shirt so fast in his life, pushing it off her shoulders before she quickly shrugged it off. She did take her mouth from his to pull a silk camisole off, leaving her upper body clad only in a see-through black bra.

She was back in his arms, her small breasts pressed to his chest, her nipples driving him crazy as they abraded his sensitive skin.

"Finn," she whimpered as she ran her hands over the divots of his lower back, going lower to grab his ass to pull him tighter against her center.

He trailed kisses, sucking and nipping, down her neck and chest and the swell of her upper breast before finally sucking her distended nipple into his mouth through the silk of her bra. He worked over both breasts, sucking and pinching her sensitive flesh.

She wedged one of her hands between their thighs, working

his jeans button. The relief of his rock-hard sex being freed as the zipper came down was indescribable.

Finn expected her to go straight for it—to yank his boxers low and take him in hand. Instead, she placed one palm against his chest. She leaned back from him and watched herself trace his erection through his boxers.

Her delicate fingers were tentative, but her expression was enthralled. He didn't move, barely breathed.

Her gaze swung to his face, and she gave him a small smile with her kiss-swollen lips. "I've never touched a man before—well, his penis anyway. It's...wow. I mean, you just carry that thing around in your pants day in and day out? How distracting," she deadpanned.

His hand went down and cupped Mirren's, stalling her explorations. "You... Are... You've never had sex? I thought most people lost their virginity in high school. I didn't, but still." He winced at how inarticulate that had come out.

"It's not like it's a big deal." She was nonplused at being stopped and tried to wiggle her fingers.

He'd never thought he'd see the day when he cockblocked himself, but she was Mirren, not just some stranger from a bar. "It's a very big deal. A wonderful, important big deal."

"Are you saying we won't be moving to my bedroom? You clearly still want me." She'd managed to wrap her fingers partway around his girth and give a short pump.

"Oh God, that feels so good." Before he could stop himself, he molded her hand tighter around himself and pumped—one stroke, then four more. "Shit! No, Mir. No." He groaned as he backed away from between her legs.

"Finn, please," she whined, starting to slide off the counter to follow him.

"I want you. I can't think of anything else but getting inside your body." He scrubbed a hand over his face and down his beard. Frustrated that he wasn't going to take what she was freely offering. "This is the first night we've...touched or kissed. I've not held your hand or taken you on a date. I want you to be sure since you've never done it before. I want you to be sure that I'm the one you want."

She sighed. "You're an awfully honorable man, Finn Campbell. Do you want to do those things with me—hold hands, date, touch, kiss?"

"Everything. I want everything with you, Mirren." And he did. The woman made him grit his teeth in exasperation more often than she made him smile, but somewhere along the way, he'd decided she was his.

Her pleased smile must have meant she approved of his plan. "Is kissing still on the table for tonight?"

"Most definitely, lass." He moved back into the cradle of her legs. His pants were still undone, and she was still in her bra, and if he wasn't careful, all his good intentions of not taking her to bed would fly out the window.

"You have the clarity and color of the rarest brown diamond. Did you know that?" Finn wasn't telling tales. His artist's mind could trace her delicate features every hour of every day. She kissed his palm as his fingers discovered her face.

"I should add being a poet to your attributes."

He had no resistance to that woman's allure. He had to take several deep breaths to calm his racing heart.

You are a thirty-year-old man, for Christ's sake. Show some control.

When she began to trace his shoulders and chest, seemingly fascinated by his body, he felt his muscles swell, hoping to entice her to never stop touching him.

"Your body is a wonder, Finn. Knowing what you have

under your clothes is going to make it awfully hard to keep my hands off you."

"You're the wonder, babe." He ran one finger along her collarbone, making her shiver, before going lower and tracing a straight line directly across her nipples. Her arched back begged him for more. "I don't want you to keep your hands off me."

"Can I touch you again? Here." In case he didn't know which part of his anatomy she was referring to, she ran her thumb over the head of his sex. "Your boxers are damp here."

"Christ, baby." He clenched his jaw at how good that felt, his balls drawing tight. He wanted to tell her his dick was crying because it was being denied ecstasy but managed to say, "As much as I want to say something else, the answer is no, and the boxers stay on.

"You, though, are taking your jeans off." His fingers were already at the gold medal button, flicking it open. He watched intently as her zipper clicked down.

"And what will you do once you have my pants off?"

Her breathy question had him leaning over to take her mouth again. He couldn't get enough of kissing her. While their tongues were occupied, he dragged her jeans off her legs and dropped them on the floor.

Pulling back, he said, "I plan on slipping those tiny black panties from your body."

"And then?"

All his focus was between her legs as he drew his knuckles over the heated silk. "I'm going to lean you back on this counter and taste you like I've dreamed of doing for weeks. I want you to come apart on my tongue. I want you to scream my name when you do."

Her eyes went wide as her lips parted on a soft "yes."

He had just begun to pull her panties down when an unexpected cry of alarm sounded through the kitchen. Fiona barreled around the kitchen entry, calling frantically for her brother.

He felt Mirren stiffen in his arms at hearing his sister's voice for the first time and knew his past was about ready to fuck up his life once more.

15

—————

"Finn! Christ, Finn! It's Lyle!" Fiona slid into the kitchen, where Mirren was currently half-naked and wrapped in her brother's arms.

And she was speaking but not with her hands.

Mirren could only stare in wonder as Fiona gesticulated wildly, her arms swiftly rising and dropping to her sides.

"Calm down, Fi, and explain what this is about."

Fiona took a shuddering breath after hearing her brother's even tone. "It's Lyle. I fear he's been in a car accident. He was talking to me on the phone, and I was texting him at the same time. He was in the middle of telling me a funny story when I heard a loud noise—like...like squealing tires. I swear I heard breaking glass."

She pressed her fingers into her eyes and took a stuttering deep breath before adding, "Had I not admitted that I could hear his voice, he wouldn't have gotten so excited and called me, and maybe...maybe he would have just kept voice texting. It was stupid to tell him something like that when he was driving!"

"Enough, Fi. Focus. Do you know his location?" At Fiona's

wide-eyed expression, Finn barked, "Fiona! Do you know where he was driving? Was he close to town?"

"Yes...yes." She stammered out where she thought he was.

Mirren finally got her voice unstuck and suggested, "If he told you he passed the Fordell Firs exit, then he would have been on the M90 motorway. Jamestown Hospital is close. If he was hurt, I bet he would have been taken there." Mirren grabbed her camisole and blouse from behind her, giving Finn a polite "Excuse me" as she moved him from where he was, still between her legs, and slid off the counter.

Finn finally looked at her. "Please, Mirren. Let me sort this, and then I will try to explain. Please."

He looked as gutted as she felt, but he was right. That was not the time to get into...whatever it was. "Of course" was all she could manage. If she sounded distant, well...she bloody well was.

As she and Finn quickly dressed, Mirren wanted nothing more than to demand why they'd been lying to her, but she'd agreed to wait, and wait she would. There would be time enough for that reckoning.

Instead, she offered, "I can call Dad. Since Lyle works for the company now, MacGregor Security will have outfitted his phone with all sorts of tracking software. Even if the phone is damaged, the tracker will still work."

Fiona let out a keening cry and balled her fists into her eyes, shaking her head in the affirmative. "Please, Mirren. Please do that." The distraught woman's watery voice kicked Mirren into action.

As she ran into the dining room to fetch her phone from the purse she'd dropped on the table earlier, she heard Fiona tell her brother, "If I had just spoken to Lyle, he wouldn't have had to look at his phone screen to see my responses. I did this, Finn." Her cries were muffled. Mirren saw why when she ran back into the room, already dialing her dad. Finn had pulled his sister tight to his chest.

"We don't even know what's happened yet, Fi. Calm down. Whatever's happened, we'll get it sorted."

Her dad picked up on the first ring even though it was past eleven. "Mirren." His growly voice always made her smile—or would have if the situation wasn't so shitty.

"I'll give you the facts as quick as I can."

"Sweetheart, what the fu—"

"I'm safe. Just listen." She knew he'd immediately tracked her location to her home, which was why he wasn't losing his head.

"Tell me." Thomas MacGregor could always be counted on to remain calm under immense pressure—unless the predicament involved his wife or daughters.

"Fiona Campbell was on the phone with Lyle while he was driving on the M90 when she heard a loud noise and possibly glass shattering. A wreck maybe. I need you to track his phone."

"Already on it." Mirren could tell that he had taken the phone from his ear because she heard mad typing on his laptop. "Jo, baby, call Coll and tell him Lyle might have been in an accident. Lyle's been assigned to one of his teams. Coll will want to alert everyone else the moment we find him."

"I'm putting you on speaker for the Campbells' benefit."

"Fine. His personal phone is stationary. Ringing his work phone now."

Someone answered, but Mirren could hear only her father's side of the conversation. Fiona swayed on her feet and placed her hands on the counter as she, Finn, and Mirren strained to listen.

Mirren heard her dad say, "Barr is calling the team now. Understood. What do the police believe? One of your team is en route now. It can wait until morning. Keep us in the loop. Fine. Send me your new reservation. Yes. Change it all."

After his call ended, her dad was back on the line. "I need to call your Uncle Colly, sweetheart. Lyle is fine, but it was a car accident. Another vehicle hit him from the side at a stoplight. He said he'll need a few stitches on his forehead and he's scuffed and bruised but nothing serious."

Fiona covered her face and cried silent tears. Mirren was relieved that Lyle wasn't seriously injured. In the back of her mind, she was still reeling that Fiona could speak.

"It will be a few hours before he's back on the road to Edinburgh, but I'm sure he'll take a moment to reach out to Fiona. If she gets a message from a restricted number, that would be Lyle."

Mirren almost forgot to ask, "Did he tell you how the accident happened?" Fiona's head jerked up at her question, confirming that she could not only speak but hear as well.

"We're looking into it." *Translation: it might be work related.*

That was concerning but not related to the Campbells, so Mirren wouldn't share her thoughts. "I understand. Thanks, Dad."

There was a beat of silence before her father asked, "Everything is good with you, Mir?"

Crap. Her dad had always been so sensitive to her moods. "Of course. I'm relieved Lyle will be fine. I'll talk to you and Jo soon. Give kisses to my sweet Gray."

More silence. "You aren't telling me something, and I don't like it." To be loved by a parent as deeply and completely as her dad loved her was a blessing and, at times, like right that moment, a curse.

"I'm only tired, Dad, I promise."

Ignoring her words, he spoke to his wife, who must have

been next to him. "Call Mary. Your mother can check on things until you're well enough to travel."

Josephine's voice was muffled but clear enough to hear. "Thomas, babe, you've forgotten again that Mirren is an adult. You agreed to let Mir fly free as long as she agreed to let you know the minute she might need you."

That statement was clearly meant to be the stepmother's version of a verbal spanking. Jo knew Mirren was keeping things from her father and wouldn't cover for her much longer.

"I would love it if Grandma Mary came to visit—and Jo, if Mom finds out you've been sick and haven't let her watch Gray, she'll be hurt."

"Are you threatening me with the wrath of Aileen?" Jo asked, humor tinging her voice.

"It isn't a threat if I mean it, Mrs. MacGregor. I love you guys. Talk to you tomorrow, okay?"

"Not okay," her dad replied, bullheaded as always. Jo, who was a realist, said, "Kisses and hugs, Mir," before hanging up.

Mirren sighed and set her phone on the cold kitchen counter before looking at her houseguests. Though there was a height difference and, noticeably, one was feminine while the other was masculine, their wide eyes and identical leery expressions screamed "related."

"Please let me know in the morning if you speak to Lyle. I'm exhausted and turning in. Finn, you probably have a lot of things to discuss with your sister. I'm obviously out of the Campbell loop. I'm sure there are reasons for the subterfuge, but frankly, your level of deception is beyond me to comprehend tonight."

Mirren tried to harden her heart against Fiona's pleading look and slowly leaking tears. She was almost free of the kitchen when Finn's pained whisper reached her ears.

"Mirren. Please."

She cared for Finn and his sister. Their situation, whatever it was, was really hurting her. They'd had a camaraderie of sorts, a friendship, respect. Or she thought they had.

Mirren was crushed that she'd been so...wrong. The truth of the matter was that she loved her job and her life in Edinburgh, but she desperately missed her family. When Fiona and Finn had moved in, it had started to feel like she was building a new family for her home away from home.

She did know that she was too tired and emotional to face anything that night. Without turning around, she just shook her head in the negative and continued to her room.

16

———

The patrons would be asking to see her collection in a matter of months, and what did she have to show them?

Mundane pastorals and feel-good snatches of real life. A little girl sniffing flowers by a pond, for the love of God!

Boring.

Tedious.

Dull.

She kept spinning in slow circles until her head felt fuzzy and her body swayed with dizziness.

And still...still...

She stopped and stared at the painting she hated most. It was supposed to represent hope or some such bullshit emotion.

She fucking despised it.

"I could kill you for this one alone, but we both know they're all equally pathetic."

She picked up the wickedly sharp knife she'd brought in from the garden shed and was about to slash the canvases to ribbons when a whimper worked its way into her abused eardrums. The pounding cacophony of her heavy breathing and the ever-present *thrum of whispered words weren't enough to keep the inhalation from penetrating.*

She'd heard the whispers for years. Some of her favorite moments involved lying in a dark, quiet room and talking back to them.

Unfortunately, she couldn't focus enough to see what her dark demons were trying to tell her.

Because of that fucking whimper.

Pausing, she lowered the knife and spun on her heel. "Oh, you don't like that, do you? Well, I don't care, hag."

She let the knife graze the outside of the canvas, the sharp tip flaking off a bit of dried paint.

Maybe she was being shortsighted. Maybe she was being too hasty.

"Think. Think. Think." Turning her head, she narrowed her eyes on the disgusting creature staring back at her.

She could count on only herself. What did she know with certainty?

One: there wasn't enough time to create a new collection, and the pathetic museum judges weren't ready to embrace her true style of art.

Two: the art in that room was passable but would never win.

Three: there were too many talented artists vying for what she wanted.

Four: she needed less competition.

Four and a half: she needed less competition from oil painters.

"I think you're right. This once." She walked back to the table and, without giving her intention away, slammed the knife, point first, as deep as she could penetrate the ancient surface, years and years of paint residue slowing the blade's progress.

She felt a smile begin to stretch her lips as she looked at the embedded weapon. Now, that was art.

Sighing, she gave the incompetent layabout one more glare for good measure before she left the stifling room.

"I need to stop staring at this...this travesty"—she swept both hands, indicating the room at large—"and focus on a different path."

17

———

For almost nine months, Finn and his sister had been living back at their lonesome home in St Margaret's Hope, where only the rare curlew or lonely fox wandered. Eight and a half months of torturing himself with images of Mirren's betrayed expression had left him feeling haunted.

He and Fiona worked from sunup until sundown and regularly longer than that. Each of them was trying to forget the ones they'd left in Edinburgh.

After Lyle's accident, Fiona wouldn't listen to any reason. She was convinced that the cause of his accident was his being distracted while reading her messages. Had she just spoken to him out loud, he would never have been hurt. It had been terrifying watching her spiral.

She was shutting down like she had the night he'd found her on the living room floor. She needed help. The kind he couldn't give. She wanted to run. Run from Edinburgh, from Lyle, and from Mirren. Mirren knew Fiona could speak, and his sister knew the other woman would expect an explanation.

Fiona said that the moment her mind touched on the

memory, panic would flood her body, and her mind would yell at her to retreat, to run and hide.

After Mirren had left them alone after speaking to MacGregor that night, Fiona had begun signing to him, her mouth clamped in a grim line. It had been like she couldn't physically make it move to speak.

Finn had panicked. He had known that he couldn't go through years of getting only half his sister. He remembered trying to reason with her.

"I'm calling your therapist. I'll set up a video chat. She'll help you see that things are far from the catastrophe you're painting them to be."

"I'll see her the moment we're home. I promise. I just need you to take me home. Now. I'll start packing."

"Surely, you can't mean for us to sneak away in the middle of the night like criminals. And unthankful ones at that. How would that make Mirren feel?"

"You saw her face. We lied to her for weeks. How do I tell... What do I... What would she think if she knew?"

Finn had grasped her shoulders. He remembered thinking her body was buzzing, desperate with the need for flight.

"Christ, Fi! She doesn't have to know everything, but even if she did, she would think what I think. That you are the bravest woman I know. That you're beautiful and talented and a fighter."

She had stilled for a moment, her sawing breaths easing until she'd asked, "And Lyle?"

"Are you telling me that you love a man who is fickle? A coward? Would he turn from you because something horrible happened to you against your will? Is that who Lyle is? Because if it is, you're better off without him."

"He is none of those things, Brother." She'd squeezed her eyes shut. A full minute had passed before she'd shaken her head and sighed in defeat. Her forehead had thunked against his chest, and her shoulders had curved in.

He'd known before she'd spoken. He'd known what she would ask of him. And he'd known he wouldn't tell her no.

"I can't do it. Not yet. I need space."

"What does space look like to you?"

"Let's pack up what we can tonight and have a moving company get the rest. We can finish our exhibit pieces at home."

When he hadn't responded, she'd taken a step back so she could see his face. "I know I'm asking a lot."

"It isn't living here or the exhibit. It's..." He'd hesitated, so Fiona had finished for him.

"Mirren. I know. God, Finn, I'm sorry. How about you help me get home, and you come back here. I know we've never been apart, but it wouldn't be forever, and Mirren is amazing and good for you. I understand that."

"I won't leave you." That, of course, had been final.

He'd decided not to disclose what Mirren had shared earlier about the reporter possibly researching their past. He had figured that if they were moving home anyway, it would only upset Fiona further.

So that had been that. He'd run from Edinburgh for the second time in his life and hated the flight all over again but for very different reasons.

Finn turned slowly in his shop and looked at the tables, cubbies, and walls covered with all the pieces for his exhibit.

He'd worked so many hours the past several months that he'd managed to fill jewelry orders for several high-end jewelers. An American bride had even ordered matching wedding bands for her and her husband.

Work was well, business was well, but he was so heartsore that his chest ached night and day with it. He missed Mirren. He wanted her to see what he'd created and give him her opinion. He wanted to touch her again. He wanted to hear her snarky comebacks.

He wanted his mouth on her neck and his hands in her hair.

He wanted her to have waited for him.

He wanted her forgiveness for putting his sister before her.

Christ...how he wanted.

Finn heard the door open and close behind him, the slight draft ruffling his drawings and haphazard invoicing system. He should have taken Mirren up on her offer to bring him out of "the cave wall drawing era" and update his website.

As she tended to do, his sister was prowling around his workroom, poking and prodding his work. "With the exception of the *Unkindness*, this is the best work you've ever done, Finn." She walked over to his desk and sat on top of a pile of papers, ignoring that she was making an even bigger mess of his "filing system."

He agreed with her though. The collection was all bronzes and coppers and browns—the latter reminded him of the beautiful, varying shades of Mirren's hair. All of the pieces revolved around the ancient Scottish targe shield. Some were decorated simply—gold circles with carved patterns and brass pins. The metal sculptures set on the floor and spare counters were cohesive yet individual statements.

For other pieces, he'd spent days carving miniature heraldry symbols that included animals, mainly stags and unicorns. Each piece of his jewelry, which included cuffs, bangles, chokers, earrings, delicate chains, and bold rings, was dark and mysterious—gold and brass, brown cassiterite mixed with brown diamonds. He'd spent a small fortune on the stones, but nothing but the best would do for that collection.

"It is," he finally replied. "I would say the same of your latest work." Finn wasn't complimenting her for nothing. Fiona was a master of capturing human moments, everyday moments that persuaded people to sit and just look. Her paintings entranced. He was so proud of her. It wasn't because they were related; she was that talented.

Her newest collection was all scenes from Edinburgh, which Mirren had encouraged. Many of the scenes depicted sadness, loneliness, violence, poverty, or the seediness of life after dark.

There were haggard mothers holding hands with their small children, each lined up behind her like starving ducklings; a man with dark, hopeless eyes having a smoke on his stoop; drug deals; and prostitution. It was brilliant, but it was real and raw, and it made his chest ache.

There was one painting, though, that made Finn more emotional than the others. "My favorite is the man kneeling in a puddle in the pouring rain to propose to his girlfriend." It showed hope. It showed that his sister still had hope for something better for herself.

Fiona's lips pursed, her paint-stained nails drumming against her thighs. "*Grey Chances.* That's the name of that one."

Finn only nodded. He wanted a chance for them both, no matter the color. "We have to go back soon." To Edinburgh. Finn was burning to go back.

"Mirren emailed me this morning. She's offered her home again while we finish our pieces and work with our exhibit coordinators. It's a kind offer, but then she's one of the kindest people I know."

"I see." It took every ounce of Finn's control to unlock his jaw and fists at the mention of the woman he'd left. "I've been looking at a house near Mirren's to lease. I don't want to take advantage."

"I agree. Have you spoken to Mirren?" Fiona knew he hadn't.

"Have you spoken to Lyle?" he countered. Before she could respond, he clarified, "I don't mean through text."

"Not once. He stopped texting weeks ago. He probably moved on months ago. I hope I don't run into him. I miss him."

Before he could stop himself, he asked, "And you think I don't miss Mirren?" He spun around so she couldn't see his expression, clasping the window frame and staring at...nothing.

"There's no hiding our pain from each other, Brother. There never has been. I'm ashamed every day that I took you from her."

Her raspy inhalation meant she was fighting tears. He closed his eyes to the roiling waves of the ocean and tried to block out her pain because he *could* feel it. That day wasn't the first time he'd wished their close bond to hell.

"The night Dad did what he did to me, I think most of me died... I think a part of me wanted all of me to die. Did I ever tell you"—she paused—"when he was holding me down, he told me if I kissed him, he would let me go."

"Fi. Don't." Finn kept staring blindly at the distant waves.

"I did it. It wasn't a simple kiss. It was my first kiss. My only kiss," she huffed, a noise that sounded an awful lot like disbelief. "He lied. Of course, he lied. Therapy has shown me that I hold the most shame because of that kiss because I gave it freely."

"You gave nothing freely," he said harshly.

She ignored his outburst. "I planned on kissing Lyle the minute I saw him. He wanted to kiss me too. But then the accident and the crushing guilt that my dishonesty might have been the cause of his distraction... God, Finn. The thought of staying and seeing him and kissing him with lips that had known only my dad's... Christ, but I couldn't do that to him."

Finn heard himself expel a breath of mourning and regret. Fiona *never* spoke of that night. He wanted to scrub his mind of the image she'd painted, even knowing that the "kiss" wasn't the worst of it.

He kept his back toward her. He didn't want to move in case she needed to say more and that was the only way she could.

"I did want to die. Forever, it seemed like, but I came back to myself for both of us. I wouldn't make it without you, and I think you wouldn't fare well without me. You've spent all these years in purgatory with me." He heard a thump like she'd smacked her chest. "Not dead but not living either. I've done that to us."

"No, Fi. You are the other half of me. There is nothing you could ask of me that I wouldn't give freely."

"I know, damn it, and that's the problem. There is not a brother more deserving of love than you. I've held you back. Knowingly. It's been an unacceptable ask for years, and yet, I kept asking it of you. I'm done doing that."

"Okay," he drew the word out slowly, not sure what that meant or what it would mean for their future.

"Thomas MacGregor called me a few days ago."

That had him swiftly spinning around to look at his secret-keeping sister. "And you're just now mentioning it? Christ, Fi. That's bullshit." He'd been reaching out to Mirren sparingly, praying each time that she would keep responding, and she had been—in a responsible, concise, businesslike way.

She held up a hand. "No need for a mantrum. I'll explain."

Finn couldn't help a snort of amusement, which felt damn good after the last few minutes. "You sound like Mirren."

"She is a smartass and the reason why I took a chance with Smith Gallery. So I'll take that as a compliment."

"Why did MacGregor call you?" *And not me*, he wanted to add, but if it sounded childish in his mind, it was sure to sound worse out loud.

"Thomas told me to quit fucking around in the Orkneys and

get my ass back to Edinburgh. He said to tell my idiot brother to sell our house here and make the move permanent—if you want a chance with his daughter and if I want a chance with Lyle."

Finn was shocked speechless. He couldn't even close his gaping mouth. Had MacGregor meant that he might not have ruined everything with Mirren?

She chuckled. "I know. I had the same reaction."

"Was that all he said?"

"Hardly. He told me that I might as well speak to him because he knew I could."

"Jesus. He came on strong." Finn liked that the man didn't shy away from sensitive topics. "Did you?"

Fiona grinned. A full grin that made her eyes sparkle. "Yes. I just did it!" She threw her arms wide in glee.

"My God, Fi." He heard the wonder in his voice. "This is... I don't... This is huge. I'm beyond proud of you. What else did he have to say?"

She didn't answer right away. Eventually, she shrugged and said, "He said he knew about what Dad did to me and why we fled Edinburgh." As if she hadn't just dropped a grenade, she rushed on. "A neighbor found him and called for an ambulance. Thomas found a police report. The woman who called it in said she heard a woman screaming. His pants were still around his ankles, and there was...blood..."

She didn't finish. She didn't have to. "Why would he fucking tell you that?" Finn felt his hands fist, picturing how satisfying it would be to plow them into MacGregor's face.

"He said that no one deserves an ounce of truth from me except what I'm willing to give. He said, and I quote, 'It's about time you take the power out of that dead bastard's hands. He's dead, but you're still hiding from him.' He isn't wrong, and I think it's time we both take our lives back, Brother. Oh, he also said he and Mr. Barr dislike Mirren's boyfriend."

18

Mirren was a wreck. Thank you, God and all his angels, that she was crazy booked with appointments.

The Campbells were due back that day.

According to "sources," a.k.a. Josephine MacGregor, the twins had bought a country home and were permanently moving to the city.

Their house was a five-minute walk from Mirren's. She wasn't exactly freaking out about the close proximity—not exactly—but her armpits had been breaking out in random sweats for the past five days since she'd heard the news.

She'd been prickly for months from the embarrassment of having the man she'd been five minutes away from taking to her bed sneak out of her house in the middle of the night, but that didn't mean she couldn't behave professionally.

For months, she had dutifully updated the Campbells on any museum exhibit information. She'd spent the last few weeks rearranging the Smith Gallery to hold the siblings' work according to the specifications they'd sent.

Everything was running smoothly and right on schedule. She'd been dating a banker who was equal parts handsome and funny. He was a little too funny at times, truth be told, but still, he was perfectly perfect.

Her MacGregor dad hated him. Her Morrow dad was ambivalent, which wasn't a point in Brandon's favor. Her uncle Colly was having him followed by one of Lyle's team.

It was not exactly smooth sailing, but she was a pro at bluffing, and right then, her bluff was projecting a confident woman. Finn would never know how deeply he'd hurt her or how much she missed him.

Her dad had warned her against passing judgment without knowing all the facts. Well, she hadn't been given any facts, so she'd been in a free-for-all judgment zone for months.

Mirren had thought she and Finn were tiptoeing around boyfriend-girlfriend territory, almost lovers, at least…friends.

Waking up to find the house empty and reconciling to herself that she and Finn were none of those things had snatched her unbiased thoughts and tossed them in the bin with the other garbage.

She wasn't some mopey, limp dish towel. A man didn't dictate her emotional state, her success, or her self-worth, but Christ, his kiss-then-abandon episode had rocked her foundation.

Even if she denied that her feelings had been hurt, Mirren's dads and moms wouldn't believe her. Those four had been breathing down her neck for months. Despite the parental overkill, and that included her uncle Coll and her aunt Cat, she had at least managed to snag a boyfriend.

It was a semiplatonic relationship. Brandon was a good kisser, but he was nowhere near as good as a certain grumpy redheaded metalworker. Mirren had had plenty of sleepless nights reliving the man's angles and ridges.

Finn's body had been sculpted in a forge. His roughened hands had felt masterful against her soft skin. He had fit so perfectly between her legs. It was embarrassing how easily she could get herself off from the memory alone. Recalling how he'd pumped his rigid sex through her fingers had her squeezing her thighs tight.

She'd practically begged him to take advantage of her that night, but the man took honor as seriously as her fathers. *Damn him.* It was honestly a blessing that they hadn't gone further. If they'd shared something so personal and he'd still run back to St Margaret's Hope, she would have had a lot more than hurt feelings.

Sighing at where her thoughts were, or rather, who her thoughts were about, she fiddled with the few contracts and invoices lined up precisely on her desk. She had a meeting with a museum exec to make sure Smith Gallery would be ready for the exhibition in a few weeks. It was a formality. Mirren would never drop the ball on something so important for the Smiths or the Campbells.

Her cell rang. She barely held in a groan when she saw Brandon's name flash on the screen—not the right reaction to indicate their relationship was headed in the right direction.

She and Brandon had been casually dating for four months by then, and she could tell he was getting tired of her unenthusiastic responses to his wandering hands.

It was unfair of her to judge his limp attempts. He was taking his cues from her, after all, but Finn...took. He dominated her mouth and body. Breathing became optional. Only his tongue against hers and his teeth nicking her skin mattered.

"Christ, Mirren. Get ahold of yourself," she chided.

Gearing up a bubbly, friendly voice, she answered. "Hi, Brandon. This is a midmorning surprise." There was no lie in her greeting. She didn't say it was a good surprise.

"Hey, babe." *Cringe.* "Some of the higher-up partners at the bank invited me to a casual dinner tonight. Employees are encouraged to bring their spouses or significant others. I was hoping it wasn't too short of notice and you could meet me after work."

He sounded so hopeful. *Crap.* She'd been avoiding any and all work events on the off chance that they wouldn't work out. She could kiss her plan of consuming whisky and caramels in bed that night—while obsessing over Finn settling into his new house—goodbye.

At her hesitation, he added, "I'd really like to introduce you to a few of my friends. No one believes you exist." He huffed a laugh, but it was too easy to hear the disappointing truth in his words.

That added guilt to her ongoing disinterest. She had to swallow a third sigh before answering. "Of course, I can make it. Sounds fun. Text me the time and place, and I'll meet you there."

He was quiet for a beat too long. Clearly, he hadn't expected her to agree. *You and me both, buddy.* Guilt was a bitch. Brandon was a great guy, and if she'd never met Finn, they might have really hit it off—but she had met Finn...touched Finn.

"Oh, wow, that's great, babe. I can't wait!"

Hanging up, she hung her head. "Mirren, Mirren, Mirren," she chastised herself. She couldn't even talk on the phone with her boyfriend for two minutes without thinking about Finn, or as Jo preferred to call him, The Runner.

Well, The Runner would be returning to Edinburgh that day, permanently, if her dad's intel was to be believed. She'd asked him how he was in the know of Campbell's plans. His answer had been as annoying as only he could have made it.

"Nosiness doesn't become you, Mir."

She rolled her eyes even though he wasn't there to appreciate it. She rounded her desk and went into the main gallery room to wait for the museum rep, Mr. Tall. Mirren prayed he wasn't a stodgy biscuit.

There were only two weeks until the exhibit. She'd sent out several press releases that morning to begin garnering a buzz. A short write-up about the siblings and their art styles had been added.

Since Finn worked with metal, she knew he would gain a lot of attention. It wasn't often that a jewelry maker had an exhibit, and because his would also include metal sculptures and framed sketches, it would have all the bells and whistles for a pretty spectacular show.

The museum judges would have three weeks to view all of the participants' exhibits and a final week to pick the winners for each media style. Smith Gallery was in a third-week primo spot.

The pieces would be installed a few days before the show and covered so no curious eyes could catch a glimpse of them. Speaking of curious eyes, Mirren had been hearing rumblings around the art world in Scotland that Lance had become a real nuisance.

He'd been caught snooping at an old farm outside Glasgow. A painter in the competition had been working at his patron's country estate over the summer. According to one of Mirren's friends—a friend who worked at a gallery in Glasgow—the police had been called, but Lance had gotten off with a stern talking-to when he'd convinced everyone that he had just let his excitement at meeting the artist overcome his good sense to call first.

"So sleazy," Mirren said to herself. She still couldn't believe she'd gone out with him. Interrupting her thoughts, a smartly dressed, very rotund, very short man marched in. The grin on his face instantly made a grin form on her own.

Walking forward and extending her hand, she asked, "Mr. Tall?"

"Of course, dear! Did my stature not give me away?"

She hadn't expected their meeting to be amusing from the get-go. Chuckling, she introduced herself. "Mirren MacGregor—and whatever do you mean?" She made a point of looking down her nose at him. He was a good three inches shorter than her five-foot-five-inch frame.

Shaking her hand enthusiastically, he said, "Pleasure to meet you, Miss MacGregor. I've been hearing good things about you, young lady."

"Mirren, please, and only good things? Gracious, I need to up my game if I hope to achieve mediocrity."

His eyes sparkled at the banter. "Call me 'Tom,' then. My wife has called me 'TT' for the past forty years, but I'll spare us both that. She says it's only my initials, but her favorite food is tater tots, and as I do kind of resemble the crispy little brown nuggets, well..." he trailed off, grinning.

The meeting was productive and quick. Mirren went over Fiona's and Finn's exhibits and showed Tom the spaces they would occupy. She gave him the folder she'd prepared with copies of the press releases that had gone out and those that would be posted in the future. She'd included the invitation that several elite members of the art world would receive to attend the preshowing before the exhibits were open to the public, which the judges would also attend.

Mirren tapped the cream-and-gold invitation with her fingernail. "That invitation isn't just for your review, Tom. I would be thrilled if you and your wife felt like putting on your Sunday best and joining us." She hadn't planned on inviting him, but he was so genuinely enjoyable, not to mention intelligent and quite knowledgeable about art. The Smiths had given her a handful of invitations to give out at her discretion. Her parents were getting four of them.

The look of shock and pleasure painting Tom's face pleased Mirren immensely. "Listen, TT, if you have a better offer for the evening, you won't hurt my feelings," she teased.

"My Bonny and I would be thrilled to accept," he answered, only slightly flustered. "My little brother will be in attendance, and I would quite enjoy annoying him. He's a renowned art critic. Don't ask for his name, young lady, for you won't get it. He doesn't go by 'Tall.' The dandy doesn't enjoy the irony as much as I do," he shared.

Mirren was startled to hear of Tom's connection, but her learning his brother's name wouldn't have altered her invitation. She had no doubt that his brother would be wowed by the Campbells.

"I look forward to you meeting my sweet Bonny and her, you. I need to get to my next appointment, Miss MacGregor." He hesitated before finishing. "I wasn't supposed to say anything, but, in good conscience, I have to say *something*. Put extra security on the art installations. There has been a bit of an accident with one of the participants' paintings and...fire."

Mirren was floored. "What? Like, someone purposely set fire to an artist's work?"

He sighed, and his shoulders curved forward from divulging such a heinous crime. "The investigation isn't complete. It looks as though it was deliberate. There have been a few other incidents, all minor in their way, but...unfortunately, the timing is suspect.

"A potter withdrew from the competition when pictures of him cheating on his wife with their barely of age nanny were leaked on the internet. Another painter from Portree in Skye was in a terrible car wreck a few months back and would never be able to complete the number of paintings needed for a true exhibit."

Mirren felt the hair on the back of her neck begin to rise. "Extraordinarily suspect. I agree."

"There have been a few other things here and there. The museum bigwigs don't want to cause a panic, but I'm of a mind that one should be nothing but panicked."

She grasped Tom's hand. "I agree with you. Thank you, Tom. Really. Thank you. I won't panic, but I will discuss the need for added security with Kain and Lillias."

"Ah, an intelligent giantess, then."

His teasing made her smile despite the disturbing revelation.

"Your Campbell twins are quite the mysterious artists. There are a few online articles and pictures but so few that many are practically salivating for the Smith event. I admit, I am beyond elated to finally lay eyes on them. You've made this old man's day, lassie."

His deepened Scottish burr was precious. "You won't be disappointed with either of them, and neither will your brother." Mirren couldn't help the smug smile that graced her mouth. No matter her personal feelings, Finn and Fiona were one brother and sister duo that she would bet on to win every day of the week.

"I need to get going, but you, Mirren MacGregor, have been quite a find. My Bonny will love you."

"I suggest you call your lovely wife on your way to your next appointment and let her know she has carte blanche on your American Express. Black-tie gowns aren't cheap, TT."

19

She had been hauling boxed paintings downstairs for what seemed like hours. The lazy slut upstairs had finally finished making some decent changes to the final two, and since they'd finished drying, she could get them boxed as well.

She wasn't a fan of physical labor, but she also wasn't about to allow anyone into her private space. The art world had a perception of her, and it was all landscapes and warmth. They couldn't handle her real works.

The art she was forced to exhibit as her own made her stomach roil with nausea.

It was unfortunate that a few of her competitors had dropped from the competition, but seriously, if a smidge of pressure had made them turn tail, that wasn't her fault.

Some of the quitters might have had a bit of help making their decisions to bow out thanks to her persuasive ways.

A few of the competitors didn't even matter to her—they weren't even in her field—but it had felt good to focus on hurting someone besides herself for a change.

The voices liked the chaos her actions created. She'd had to hide how much their praise affected her. Had they known, they would have been mean again. Already, they were whispering amongst themselves.

That meant the worst punishments were coming.

She shook the thought from her head. Worrying about it never made it less terrible or stopped it from happening. Her life hadn't been normal since "the accident."

Seeing that the paintings were downstairs, her patron gallery would send a truck to fetch them, which would give her time to surprise one last competitor.

And it just happened to be her biggest competition.

"Why are dirty little secrets so yummy?" She practically skipped up the stairs, she was so excited. Time to pick out the perfect cocktail dress for her competitor's big night.

She wouldn't miss the secret unveiling for the world. The voices in her head were chatting excitedly. She wouldn't let them down. She couldn't let them down.

20

Finn had been surveilling Mirren's home for the past two hours like the worst sort of stalker. Ever since his sister had told him that Mirren was dating, his temper had been lethal. Logically, he knew she had every right to date, but the night they'd kissed, the same night he'd run, he'd thought of her as his.

"Damn it," he growled and kicked another rock down the narrow lane that ran in front of her house. He had already tried the front door, knocked, and even rung the bell...three times. She must have been out.

He should have still been home unpacking like Fiona was, but he couldn't focus. He'd at least gotten his art moved into his new workroom, a small converted garden shed behind the main house. He had only some tweaking left to do on a few sculptures, so he didn't need to unbox everything.

His sister had been organizing the kitchen when he'd left. She was doing anything and everything to keep herself busy. They were both nervous about the next morning's "meeting."

Mirren had emailed Fiona that afternoon to explain that some of the artists' work had been tampered with and that a few artists had even been bothered. A cheating scandal had been outed on social media for one unfortunate artist, and another had been in a car wreck. One poor artist had had a fire set in his studio. At least the fire hadn't gotten everything. Several pieces were salvageable with minor restoration. Two were destroyed, but luckily, the artist had taken pictures of everything and the museum would allow them to be included.

Mirren had asked that they keep their art in a secure room for the time being and possibly even put up cameras and an alarm. Thirty minutes after Fiona had read him the email, MacGregor had called Finn.

Finn had answered the call and heard, "Campbell."

Finn had responded in kind. "MacGregor."

"Mir called. Said you need security. Coll is having Lyle head your way in the morning. He's already gathering the supplies."

Christ, but Mirren's father was overbearing. It was annoying that Finn liked him so well. Still... "You didn't need to do that. I am quite capable of buying and installing what's needed." A grunt was the only indication that he'd heard.

"Is your sister close?" Finn had said she was. "Put me on speaker."

He had gotten his sister's attention. "Fi, come here, please. MacGregor wants to bark more orders at us." He'd grinned at her raised brows when he'd waved the phone in the air.

"Lyle is coming in the morning to install security. Finn will be asking Mirren to come as well. You will explain your past to them. As little or as much as you please. You won't rest easy until you do, and you know it."

Fiona had gasped and paled, grabbing his hand for support, but she hadn't outright said no.

MacGregor had cleared his throat. "My Josephine had something happen to her once when she was a teenager. Therapy helped. It took her years to tell anyone. I'm only telling you this because speaking of it, even a bit of it, changed her life for the better. I'm done asking you to fix your shit, Fiona."

Fiona had huffed a disbelieving breath. "Good grief, Thomas, we've only arrived in Edinburgh today!"

Fiona had told him that she spoke out loud to MacGregor, but hearing her do it himself had been something else.

"I know you haven't spoken to Lyle or texted him. I asked Coll. It's done now. You can call and thank me tomorrow." He'd hung up without a goodbye.

Finn and Fiona had stared at each other for minutes without saying a word. She could have canceled the next morning. Finn had expected her to cancel. Instead, she had said, "Well, that's that then. I'm going to unpack my clothes, and you need to direct the people delivering the furniture."

Nothing else had been said the rest of the day. MacGregor might be an irritating sonofabitch, but he had given Finn the excuse he'd desperately needed to visit Mirren. Yes, he could have called or texted, but he felt asking in person was better.

He just wanted to see her, which was how he found himself circling Mirren's property. He'd considered the fact that MacGregor might even then be watching Finn's pathetic meandering. Even that couldn't force him to tuck tail and head home before laying eyes on Mirren.

She might have been on a date. He bared his teeth at the vision of her with another man. Disgusted with himself, he was about to reconsider his decisions and turn back when he saw lights and heard the crunch of tires. He hoped it was Mirren but equally hoped it wasn't. Hanging out at the end of her drive wasn't a great look for him.

He froze as her headlights beamed across his body. Mirren's car instantly came to a stop. He waved weakly, hoping her window was down enough to hear his pathetic "It's me."

She crept forward and rolled her window further down. "Finn?"

He sighed at how badly their interaction was going already. "It is. Might I have a word, Mirren? I'll follow your car up the drive. I only need a minute of your time."

She was parallel with him then. It killed him to see her normally expressive eyes hooded. Her fists were gripping the steering wheel tightly. She was fighting fight or flight hard. Her generous personality finally won. *Thank God.*

"I have a few minutes," she said evenly before driving on to the house.

Finn stuck his hands in his pockets and followed like a chastised child. He mentally gave himself a stern talking-to. He wouldn't make their conversation awkward. He wouldn't make it difficult. He would ask Mirren to join him and Fiona the next morning and accept her answer with grace.

She held all the cards. He had wronged her. He would argue that it hadn't been intentional. But hadn't it been?

She parked and took her time retrieving her things before stepping outside the car to join him. Christ, she was more beautiful than he remembered.

"Mirren."

"Mr. Campbell."

Ouch. "Why are you getting home so late?" *Idiot, Finn!*

"I don't think that's your concern." She tossed her bag on the hood of her car and crossed her arms over her chest, giving him a look that expressed just how unimpressed with him she was.

"Were you on a date?" *What happened to not making it awkward?*

"Goodnight, Finn."

She grabbed her bag and was about to walk away. "Wait! Mirren, please wait. I wanted to ask you something." He scratched his fingers through his overlong hair, wishing he could start over.

She paused midstep but didn't turn around. "Please come to my house tomorrow morning at eight-thirty. Fiona would like to speak to you and Lyle."

Mirren slowly pivoted until she was back to carefully watching him. Silent. Unsmiling.

He missed her smile.

When she didn't ask any questions, he started to sweat. "I didn't want to leave you all those months ago."

"You did though. Looking back, would you do anything different?"

His chest ached, and he dropped his chin to his chest, defeated. He didn't want to answer that, but he would because she deserved at least honesty from him. "I would." When her lashes fluttered wildly, he knew she was trying not to cry. "Please, Mirren. There are things you don't know. Things I hope my sister shares with you tomorrow. Please. Please come. I would never have hurt you if I had had any other choice."

She shook her head, like she couldn't believe what she was about to say. "I'll come. We still have to work together as long as your sister sells through Smith, and I'm committed to making your exhibits the best they can be for the competition. It makes sense to get over any awkwardness."

Finn dragged his rough fingers through his beard, strangely agitated that she'd agreed. He had wanted her to but not just to "get over any awkwardness." The silence between them wasn't a comfortable one.

He wanted to say something, anything to make her soften. Remembering some of their last words from the night he'd left, he told her, "I still want everything with you, Mirren." He held his breath as her expression of surprise morphed into one of wariness. He didn't blame her for her reticence.

He took a step back and then another, the crunch of gravel loud in his ears. "Tomorrow, then."

"Tomorrow."

He'd just turned and begun walking away when he heard "Finn." He spun around so quick that he tripped on his damn work boots. She was standing near a security light that created shadows across her face.

"I know you had a good reason for leaving. Dad told me that much, and he wouldn't lie to me." Finn didn't confirm or deny, waiting for the rest. "But...knowing that didn't make it hurt any less."

Finn closed his eyes tightly, his heart sore and sick from what he'd put her through.

"I know." He started to turn but decided Mirren would respect a direct approach, and he realized he didn't want to go one more hour without her knowing *his* truth. "I haven't forgotten your scent or taste. I'll never forget. This is your warning, lass. Tomorrow is a formality only. I plan on pursuing you until you are well and truly mine. Only mine. I suggest you remember that before you accept any more dates with men who aren't me."

21

Mirren was nervous walking up to the Campbells' door. Their new home was picturesque. The surrounding garden was lush with trees and flowers, and the shed in the back was probably where Finn had made his home shop. She wished she could enjoy seeing the property, but really, she just wanted the morning to be over.

Mirren could barely sleep the night before from worrying over that morning's meeting. She'd believed her father when he had told her that the siblings' story was bigger than the few months of bruised ego she'd endured. Still...

So, yes, she wanted an explanation from Fiona explaining the lying, but deep down, she knew that the revelations about to be shared were so much bigger than Mirren and Finn's brief kitchen counter hookup.

Then there were Finn's "caveman laying down the law" theatrics from the evening before. She'd been continuously reliving his...threats? Promises? His unapologetic display of testosterone had made her shiver. It was still making her shiver.

"You've been reading too many historical romances again, Mir," she scolded herself. She needed to read a palate-cleaning lighthearted mystery where the heroine was interested in only finding clues, not swooning over obnoxious, hardheaded, ruggedly handsome, muscular, bossy men. Except, she'd just downloaded a Viking romance where the main character was a blacksmith—a little too close to her metal sculpting obsession. *Damn it.*

As she raised her knuckles to give the front door a quick knock, she heard someone call her name. Turning, she watched Lyle jog up the walk with large bags of what were presumably security paraphernalia swinging in his hands.

He smiled, as friendly as ever, but she could see the strain around his eyes. He was as nervous as she was. They'd met for lunch a few times over the past few months as his security job had allowed, but they never spoke of the twins.

Taking a deep breath, she asked, "Are you ready?"

"No."

His honesty forced a huff of amusement from her. "Me neither." Turning to face the door again, she forced herself to give a quick knock before she chickened out. It opened so quickly that Mirren startled and took a step back, bumping into Lyle, who had moved up behind her.

Finn and Fiona were standing there staring at them, the shallow threshold the only divider between both duos. It seemed like the four of them stood gaping at one another for an hour, but truly, within seconds, Finn was inviting Mirren and Lyle in.

"We appreciate you meeting us, Mirren"—he nodded to her way before nodding to Lyle—"Lyle. Come in. Fi made scones and tea. I"—he grimaced—"folded a kitchen towel."

Mirren felt her lips twitch, but under the circumstances, she didn't let her itchy, nervous laugh escape. Hoping to break some of the mounting tension, she said, "I would love tea, Fiona.

Thank you. Finn, maybe you could tell Lyle where to put his bags."

"Oh, sure." Finn seemed relieved to have something to do since Fiona had remained quiet. "Bring them to the kitchen. I thought we might be able to use the center island as a workstation. I appreciate you picking everything up. I did tell MacGregor I'd do it."

Mirren did smile then at his obvious irritation.

"Thomas isn't much for changing his mind." Lyle shrugged, giving Fiona a fast glance before following Finn.

Fiona looked like a pale goddess with her wavy red hair draped delicately over her shoulders and back. And a very scared goddess.

Mirren gave Fiona a quick hand squeeze, whispering, "You've got this." To everyone else, she huffed a laugh. "What Lyle meant to say is Dad can be an overbearing, overstepping ass, but for all his faults, he does mean well."

Finn's stoic face cracked enough for a brief look of amusement. "So I've come to realize."

His comment made her curious to know just how interfering her father had been in the Campbells' lives.

Mirren took a moment to look at the open-concept kitchen. It was lovely and so Fiona. White walls set off the green accents and the bold shamrock-colored backsplash. Copper pots were set on the counter with a partially put-together brass-and-wood rack for the pots to hang from. She loved the idea of mixing metals.

"Your home is really lovely, you guys. I can't believe you found it so fast."

"Your father found it." Finn sighed and shook his head before continuing. "And then Josephine's mother, Mary, emailed Fi a few weeks ago to ask what her favorite color story was for kitchens. Guess what. Fiona told her white and green."

All Mirren could manage was "Hmm."

Lyle was bent over the sacks, but his shoulders were suspiciously moving up and down. "Right. Well, I would apologize for my family, but that would be a full-time job."

Shocking the hell out of everyone in the kitchen, Fiona quietly said, "You have a wonderful family. I will admit that Thomas MacGregor is an acquired taste."

She smiled shyly before she turned to put the kettle on. Mirren glanced at Lyle, who was looking shell-shocked. She knew from her dad that Lyle was aware Fiona could speak but knew nothing else. Hearing her voice for the first time must have been crazy.

Hearing it for the second time was still shocking.

Fiona seemed to have used up all her courage. She'd turned back to her tea. Her shoulders were hunched, and shivers rippled across her back. Mirren couldn't stand to see anyone going through so much distress. She glanced at Lyle. His jaw was clenched and flexing. He didn't like seeing Fiona upset either. Finn took a deep breath and took a step toward his sister.

Mirren held up a hand to stop him and went to her instead. She placed her hand on Fiona's slender arm, shocked at how stiff and cold Fiona felt.

"Fiona." When the woman turned her head slightly and made eye contact, Mirren had to swallow a gasp at how wrecked she looked. "I don't need an explanation. I don't need one word. You can speak, and I'm thankful for it. Let's leave it at that, shall we?"

Fiona's head tilted back to look at the ceiling before resettling. She seemed to stand straighter, and her fists gripping the counter's edge relaxed and fell to her sides. She shook her head.

"No. Thank you though." As she turned to face the others, she told them, "Please, take a seat at the island."

Finn went to his sister, ignoring her suggestion to sit. The two of them stood facing each other, and Mirren would swear they were communicating. The two siblings were striking alone; together, with their flame-kissed hair and beautiful faces, they were a stunning pair.

Fiona shook her head once more. "No, Finn. I have to do this on my own." In answer, he simply touched his finger to her hand before seating himself.

Once Mirren and Lyle took their seats, Fiona stood at the end of the center island. All eyes trained her way. The gathering of unshed tears in her hazel eyes glistened, making them more green than brown. Her arms were wrapped tightly around her middle.

"I want to start first by apologizing. To all of you, including my brother." As they started to shift on the barstools, about to object to needing any such thing, Fiona held up her hand. "I need to do it, and you need to hear me. Please."

The plea quieted the room once more.

"Something bad happened to me when I was sixteen, and it caused me to not... It created... I've suffered from selective mutism. My brain..."—she huffed out a frustrated breath—"it wouldn't *let* me speak. I wanted to, but the moment I tried, panic would flood my body. It was debilitating.

"It took several years before I was able to speak out loud with Finn. And only Finn. It was his idea to learn sign language. It made me appear more normal." She stopped and frowned at her twin when he started to object.

Probably because he didn't like her referring to herself as not normal. Mirren didn't care for it either.

"So, we spoke aloud and signed. In public, we signed only. It eased me," she amended, shooting Finn another look. "I've been in therapy on and off for years. It helped but...not enough. It wasn't until I met you, Mirren, and your family, and...and you, Lyle, that I started to want more from myself.

"My first apology is for Finn. I've held you back, brother mine, for years, and you've never wavered. Not once. You've loved me and protected me. Always. I needed this push, and a lot of it came from your dad, Mirren." Fiona and Mirren shared a small smile over that.

"There is no amount large enough to pay you back, Finn. You've been my best friend for thirty years and nine months. I've tried to paint how much you mean to me, Brother, but there aren't enough colors in the universe to do it justice.

"I apologize to you, Lyle, and Mirren for not coming clean the moment I knew how important you were to me. I know Thomas said it wasn't my fault you were distracted when you had your accident. Still, I refuse to believe that had you not been distracted by reading my texts, you would have seen that car before it hit you."

Mirren could see Lyle wanted to argue, but he followed the rules and didn't interrupt.

"And then you, Mirren. All those emails when I could have picked up a phone. You have a deaf cousin, and still...I didn't let you know that my issue was nothing like hers. The worst was taking my brother from you. I panicked the night Lyle was hurt. I...I...Jesus, I guess that's it. I panicked.

"It wasn't just my lies that hurt you that night. I allowed you to hurt for months afterward thinking my brother was a shit. Same for Lyle." She looked directly at the man for whom she clearly had deep feelings. "I let you think you weren't important to me when nothing could be further from the truth."

She cleared her throat and placed her hands flat on the bar, rearranging a few tea towels embroidered with flowers this way and that until they were perfectly straight. Mirren knew Fiona wanted to tell them what had happened to her as a child, but Christ Almighty, she didn't think she wanted to know. Scratch that. She knew she didn't want to know.

"Unfortunately, that was the easy part of this morning's speech." Fiona tried to chuckle, but her lips quivered until she had to press them together to stop the tremors.

Mirren couldn't help the "Fiona" that slipped from her mouth. She wanted whatever Fiona's confession was to end. Finn's rumbled "No, Mir. This is for her. She *needs* to do it" shut down further protests.

"Our mom died when we were seven. It was probably a relief to her. I wouldn't know; we weren't close. Mom and Dad fought a lot. Well," Fiona amended, "Dad fought, and Mom took it.

"Dad was a drinker—spent every dime he made from his side hustles on booze. I never remember him having a job, like a real job that you go to every day. He worked for thugs and drug pushers. We found that out when we were...what, twelve, Finn?"

"That's right."

Finn's cheeks pinkened above his beard. Mirren was crushed that he was embarrassed about their dad being a piece of crap.

"Anyway. Finn and I learned to take care of ourselves. There were a few kind restaurant owners who gave us leftovers from their kitchens at least once a week if we hung around their back alleys at closing. There was one really great grocery store manager who would give us out-of-date food if we helped take the trash out and things like that. Those were the best things to get because they were packaged and we could hide them from our dad."

Mirren's stomach was churning. If it was that hard to hear, she couldn't imagine what it had been like to live it.

"Fast forward a few years, and Finn and I were old enough to get after-school jobs. We were in a program where we only had to go to high school half a day, until after lunch since food was always a concern, and we could work the rest of the day.

"It was brilliant for a while. We had money for school supplies and, once in a while, paint for me. I told you before, Mirren"—she smiled softly—"Finn was satisfied with creating his art in his mind. I was the numpty who needed to see it.

"It was when we were sixteen that things changed. Dad started to... Finn and I noticed that he was watching me. He would come home drunk and..." Fiona looked to her brother and raised her hands up and shrugged.

Finn spoke for her. "Dad watched Fi the way no father should."

Mirren heard Lyle mutter "Christ. No."

Fiona looked relieved that her brother had said that part and continued. "We took every precaution to make sure I was never home alone. Finn walked me to school and went well out of his way to walk me to my job before going to his. On clear evenings, I would sit reading or doing homework in the cemetery close to our flat until Finn got home. I got off work before he did.

"Finn stood guard outside the tiny bathroom in the flat while I showered, and I had to sit on the toilet while he showered. He hung old sheets around my pallet on the living room floor and slept near me.

"We did try to rent a room for ourselves, but no one would let property to teenagers. A few months went by, and our precautions were working.

"The night that...the night it went wrong..."

"I worked late." Finn took over. "Later than I'd intended. It was a special party at Golden Pizzeria." He looked at Mirren, nodding his head at the question in her eyes. "Alex and Sadie hired me as a dishwasher and eventually taught me how to throw pies."

Mirren could tell that Finn had mentioned his job only to give Fiona a moment.

Glancing once more at his sister, he said, "It was cold and raining that night. Fi had to beg a seat at an internet coffee shop near our place. A lot of uni students went there. It was open all night." He nodded his head for Fiona to continue.

"Long story short, Dad must have been selling drugs to some of the students coming and going from the café that night, and he saw me through the glass. Had I not gone with him, he would have made a scene. He called me 'Brenda' when he came into the shop."

"Brenda was our mother's name," Finn added grimly. "Fi. Do you want me to finish?" She shook her head and pressed one of the tea towels to her eyes to catch a few tears that she hadn't managed to blink away.

And then, oh God, and then she told them what her father had done to her on the cold floor of their shabby flat.

Fists and kisses, bruises and blood.

Rape.

Mirren, Lyle, and Finn were all crying by that point. Fiona's own dad had raped her. When Mirren was sixteen, she'd been living like a fairy princess while the Campbell twins had been living in hell.

"I'm quite sure you both wish you didn't come this morning. If I hoped for any way to move forward with the life I want for myself, I *had* to say those things out loud to the people I care about the most."

Walking around the island, she stood before Lyle and wrapped her hand around his, which was fisted on his knee. "I ran because I felt you deserved better than a woman whose only...sexual experience, her only kiss, came from that night. I was ashamed and scared and—oh...I don't know! I thought I was saving you from bowing out."

Lyle slid off his stool and grasped Fiona's shoulders. "I will never fucking run from you, Fiona Campbell. If that bastard wasn't already dead, I'd make him wish he were. I love you. That you trusted me with this..." He pulled her close and hugged her to his broad chest. "That you trusted me that much makes me love you more."

Mirren grabbed Fiona's discarded towel and held it to her cheeks. She watched as Lyle gently lifted Fiona's chin until they could all see her face.

"Promise you will never run from me again." When she only nodded, he said, "Say the words."

"I promise."

Mirren quietly stood and went to Finn's side. He was sitting rigidly and staring out the bank of windows behind his sister and Lyle. She whispered in his ear, "Would you like to walk me outside and give these two a moment?"

Finn slowly turned his head, looking at her blankly for a second before finally coming back to himself. "Yes."

As soon as Finn stood and began to follow Mirren from the kitchen, Fiona's questioning "Finn?" whispered behind them. The siblings' closeness wasn't born only from biology but also from circumstance. They'd taken care of one another for so many years, it must have been hard to be separated.

Normally, that would have been a red flag for Mirren, but after Fiona's revelations, Mirren couldn't imagine their relationship any other way.

Mirren walked the few steps back to where Fiona was still standing before Lyle. She was watching Mirren with wide, unsure eyes, and that just wouldn't do.

Mirren enveloped the other woman's cool hand in one of hers. "Thank you for trusting me. I will never make you doubt that it was a good decision. If telling me, telling us," she amended, glancing briefly at Lyle, "helped you in any way, then

I can only be grateful. I promise to deserve your trust. Now, please, talk to Lyle while I speak with your grouchy brother." Mirren smiled and kissed Fiona's cheek.

Fiona's cheeks flushed with pleasure, and her smile made Mirren give her an answering grin. The hard part, the hardest part, was behind her. The collective relief had to be knee weakening for her. In fact, Mirren realized that she had never seen Fiona look so...light, free, unburdened.

Before Fiona could answer, Lyle spoke, looking directly at Finn. "Listen, Campbell, I need to thank you for caring so well for Fiona. I hope you'll not mind me taking over some of the duty." At Fiona's sharp inhale, Lyle's eyebrows practically rose to his forehead, and he rushed to add, "Not that you're a duty, I only meant that if you needed a strong shoulder to lean on or... or, umm, you know, Fi, a confidant."

Before his sister could answer, Finn crossed his arms over his chest and asked, "Did you remain faithful to my sister while we were in Orkney all these months?"

"I did."

"No dates even?" Finn looked skeptical.

"Finn!" Fiona protested.

To Lyle's credit, he answered without hesitation. "If I ate out, it was with my security crew or Mirren. As friends only," he quickly added. "Mirren and I are friends, but we both knew her uncle Coll wanted me to take her out on occasion to pump her for intel on her personal life and report back."

Mirren made a fair imitation of her dad's growl. "Jesus, I don't know how Aunt Cat puts up with that man."

Lyle gave Mirren a brief smile but spoke solemnly when he said, "Nine months was nothing to wait for the woman I love. There has been no one else," Lyle finished, looking directly at Fiona.

Finn nodded once, satisfied with Lyle. Mirren looked at

Fiona, who looked like she was about to swoon over Lyle's declaration. "Well, Fi, now that the strong men have everything figured out for you, I've got some work to get done this afternoon." She smiled and waved a short goodbye.

"I assume your work isn't another date," Finn said behind Mirren's back as he followed her out of the kitchen.

Mirren heard Fiona snicker, which, despite her brother's overbearingness, made her smile. "Just what I needed in my life. Another overprotective man to lead the way."

22

Finn was trying to keep his cool as he marched out of the house behind Mirren. However, his artist's eye still appreciated how the lighter streaks of her brown hair caught the sunlight as they stepped outside. She hadn't told him whether "work" was code for another date, and his need to pull her into his arms and make her tell him was beating at his chest.

He hadn't wanted to leave his sister, but that was just old habits. Their dad was dead, and good riddance. Only his memory could hurt Fiona, and she was committed to not giving her past ghosts power.

He had to be strong. He had to see his twin as something separate from himself. She was becoming stronger, braver... independent of him.

Lyle was a good man, but it was still difficult to relinquish his protective nature over his sister. Thirty years had created a habit that was proving difficult to let go of, but since Fiona had been brave enough to speak about her past, then he would be brave enough to take a step back. At least at that moment, he could focus on getting back into Mirren's good graces.

After a few more steps, he asked, "Can I walk you home? You told my sister you needed to speak with me."

She grinned at him as he came up to her shoulder so they could walk side by side. "Oh, I didn't need to talk to you about anything. I just wanted to give them some alone time."

"Still, I'd like to work some things out between us."

"The sooner you realize that I've always done exactly as I wish, the better. I learned as a child that there are all sorts of workarounds for overprotective men."

Finn felt his body tighten at her insinuation that he was *just* another man. "I don't want you to work around me."

They'd already made it to the road that led to her home when she stopped to give him her full attention. "You've made your wants clear...well, semitransparent. I'm not playing with you, Finn. I already knew from Dad that you felt there was no other course that last night but to leave me without a word, but we both know you could have emailed me...something. You could have asked me to wait for you, shown me that there was hope.

"You've been shielding your sister for years and years, and I appreciate your love and dedication. You provided what she needed without ever putting yourself first. I find that extraordinarily honorable. That doesn't mean you will dictate my life or where I choose to spend my time. I do want to explore...us. I won't commit to more until we know each other better."

"I've wished more than a thousand times that I did things differently. You're right. My need to protect my sister prevented me from reaching out once we'd left, and that's inexcusable. If I wasn't such an inexperienced asshole, I would have told you to wait for me. *Demanded* that you wait for me." He grasped one of her hands between his. "Would you have?"

She shrugged. "Perhaps, but we'll never know because you never asked."

It wasn't a no, but it wasn't a definitive yes either. He didn't say a word. He took her hand, a delicately beautiful thing compared to his metal-roughened, calloused one, and placed it against his chest.

"Do you feel how fast my heart is beating?" She gave a short nod in the affirmative. "I am committed to you. To us. You say you aren't there yet, but you will be. I won't give up until it's true."

Mirren pressed her lips together before sighing deeply. "I said I understand why you did what you did. Fiona was your priority, and she needed you more than I did that night. Understanding in my brain and understanding in my heart are two separate things. I will not commit to a man who is not wholly committed to me—no matter the circumstances."

"And you shouldn't. You deserve more. You deserve everything." He closed the distance between them until her hand was sandwiched between their bodies. "Now that Fi has a support system that includes more than me, I can and will put you first."

Mirren didn't respond right away. She gazed at him with a shrewd eye, checking for any bullshit. She wouldn't find any.

"To be decided, then," she finally decreed.

"To be decided," he agreed.

23

It was taking a toll on Mirren to act all cool and collected while the man she'd dreamed of for nights on end walked silently by her side. He wanted her back in his life. She had never wanted him to leave in the first place. She was still pissed that he'd left her—and she was ashamed she felt anything remotely like that after hearing Fiona's story.

She *had* to get over it. Could he have taken care of his sister and made sure Mirren wasn't left completely in the dark? Yes. Did she understand that Finn and Fiona's relationship had, until recently, been an isolating one, unhealthy with guilt and shame? Yes. Did she want to open her arms wide and let Finn walk right into her embrace? Yes.

Would she? Not yet. Maybe. Not completely. Holding back felt idealistic and self-sabotaging. It also felt safe.

"Can I make you dinner tonight? I have a feeling Fiona and Lyle won't be letting each other go anytime soon, and I..."—he shoved his hands in his pockets—"I don't want to let you go either."

Damn, but the man had a way about him. "Just dinner?"

The serious look he gave her sent chills up and down her spine. Distance was going to be a hard ask.

"Dinner. You committing to exclusivity with me. A kiss goodnight. Dinner and two addendums." He shrugged, like the addendums couldn't be helped.

Feeling her cheeks flush, Mirren barely managed to answer calmly. "Dinner and a kiss goodnight," she countered. "It's a bit early to jump right into exclusivity."

"Not for me."

His chiseled jaw flexed, drawing attention to the gorgeous beard Mirren was dying to scratch her fingers through. Obstinate men were clearly a woman's kryptonite because she was feeling decidedly weak in the knees and warm between her thighs at his mulish behavior.

"I understand why you left so abruptly. I do, Finn, but you could have given me something these past months. You told me that night that you wanted everything with me. If that were true—"

"Christ, Mirren," he said, interrupting. He closed the distance between them and placed his hands on her waist, anchoring her an inch shy of touching.

"It was true. It *is* true," he corrected.

"You gave me nothing, though, to make me think you hadn't changed your mind. Now you're here and trying to dictate who I date." She lifted her hands in the air, exasperated, remembering a bit late that no one could drive her anger up faster than Finn Campbell.

"I screwed up. Not for leaving—that night was a necessary retreat for Fi—but for all the rest, all the months apart. That is one of my biggest regrets. I tried to reach out. You made it clear that you didn't want to speak to me about anything but work."

"But—"

She tried to interject, but he wasn't done. "It's a poor excuse.

I should have come back and made you listen. I wouldn't have been able to tell you everything, but I could have told you something." He shook himself, as if his actions, or nonaction, were weighing on him.

"It's been my sister and me for, well, forever. You're the first thing I've ever wanted bad enough to question living in the middle of nowhere with only Fiona for company."

She expelled a gust of air when she felt Finn's fingers press firmly around her waist, his thumbs pressed tightly on either side of her jeans button.

He lowered his face until his lips barely touched the shell of her ear. "I fucked up where you were concerned. It won't happen again. Let me try."

Let me try. His deep, gravelly voice, paired with the soft bristles of his beard gently scratching her neck, had her pulse pounding.

Who was she kidding? She turned her head just enough to see his eyes—and put her mouth in line with his. She wanted to see his eyes when she told him, "I'll let you try." Relief, quickly followed by satisfaction, crossed his expression.

When she unconsciously touched the tip of her tongue to her lower lip, he moaned, and his fingers flexed. One hand slid up her back, bowing her toward his body. The other hand found her face, cupping her jaw and running a thumb over her full lips.

"Finn." Was she begging him to kiss her when, only minutes ago, she had been encouraging him to keep things simple and slow? She hadn't wanted to open herself up to the kind of hurt his first abandonment had caused or be foolish by moving too fast, yet here she was...

His thumb stilled on the pouty bow of her lower lip. She heard a low "Christ." Mirren thought he was about to ravage her mouth, but instead, she felt his hands drop and watched in stunned disbelief as he took several steps back. Confusion deepened in her brain. She somehow managed not to utter a word of protest. Her body, however, was protesting mightily.

She watched in fascinated uncertainty as Finn adjusted the sizable bulge behind his zipper. His body hadn't changed its mind, then.

"Get inside, Mir, before I add more addendums to our dinner. I'm off to home and the grocery. I'll be back at six. Should I pick up a bottle of Glenmorangie?"

She shook her head to clear the lustful cobwebs so she could discuss...grocery shopping, apparently. "My other dad, Charles, keeps me supplied. It's his favorite too." *A simple "No, I have plenty" would have sufficed, Mir. Don't become a rambler.*

He gave a short nod. Nothing else. Not even a "My boner and I are off to the store. See you in a few." She didn't move from the front door until she could no longer see the strong, sure strides of Finn Campbell. Only then did she punch in the code to her door and let herself in. A squeal of delight and a teenage-worthy giggle might have followed.

From the first moment that man had walked into her gallery and irritated the piss out of her, she'd been infatuated.

She was well more than infatuated right then.

24

Mirren was in her element, which meant her day was hectic and full of demanding customers and dramatic artists. That day, it also meant she had to field questions from the press about the upcoming gallery event.

She needed to have every item on her checklist ticked off by four because she had to shut the doors early to give the new security guards the Smiths had hired a walk-through of the gallery before heading home. Finn and Fiona were setting up their exhibits for the show the following day. The actual event was scheduled for three days after that.

The Smiths had taken Mr. Tall's advice to heart, deciding to keep round-the-clock physical security until after the big event on Friday evening. Neither Mirren nor the Smiths wanted to take any chances with the Campbells' art.

After seeing a few of the pieces via email, Mirren had no doubt the twins' fame was about to skyrocket. Fiona's popularity had been steadily growing, and Finn already had a solid fan base. His mysterious persona was simply because he refused all interviews. His website didn't even have a single picture of him.

She planned on fixing that. People enjoyed a mystery, but they needed *something*.

Once the public found out that there was not one but two artists in the family—and twins—Mirren knew it wouldn't matter if one or both of them won a spot in the museum's exhibition; their course would be set.

Of course, she was partial to their work. She had pursued Fiona relentlessly after seeing a few of her paintings online and been so thrilled when Fiona had agreed to come to Smith. And Finn—well, she'd been wearing his work for several years.

Smith Gallery would be the talk of the art world for snagging two such unique and talented artists. The press was going to be ravenous to know more about the elusive artists.

The night before at dinner, Finn had refused her suggestion to do in-person interviews, and when she'd made the suggestion to Fiona, the answer had been the same. Having dealt with all manner of artists, Mirren found their refusals disappointing but not surprising.

They were protective of their privacy for obvious reasons— more valid reasons than most. So when Finn had given her a flat no the night before while flipping crab cakes, one of her very favorite dishes, Mirren hadn't blinked an eye. It was his art and his prerogative.

Answering the last of her emails, she leaned back in her office chair and let herself remember the previous evening, the tips of her fingers pressed against her lips, barely stopping the grin wanting to break free.

True to his word, he'd gone grocery shopping and returned to her door by early evening, bags in hand.

She'd answered the door, casually leaning on the jamb, hoping her shaking limbs wouldn't be obvious. "You're here," she'd said in a ridiculously breathy voice.

"I said I would be," Finn had answered gruffly, moving past her without an invitation.

"Come in," she'd said to his retreating back. Rolling her eyes, she had followed him, wondering for the millionth time why she was attracted to annoying men.

With his normal efficiency, Finn had emptied the paper grocery bags, organizing the ingredients, which included a container of fresh crab and several mini lidded containers of spices.

He'd briefly looked at her with a grimace. "I brought my own spices," he'd confirmed. "I didn't know if you'd have everything I need."

Mirren had only nodded, wondering whether the extra dose of curtness he was vibing was because of nerves. Had he been as nervous as she had been?

"What are you making? I see crab. It's my favorite."

"I know. Crab cakes, a garden salad, homemade croutons, and chocolate chip cookies without the chips."

He must have remembered that her mom had made her a batch at her dad's cookout. *How precious*, she'd thought, barely keeping her grin in check. "I really do despise chocolate chips. Thank you for remembering. Fiona told me you do all the cooking."

"Most of it."

Good grief. She had wanted to yell "Jesus Christ, man, help me help you make this less awkward!" but settled for "Can I help with anything?"

He'd glanced at her again when she'd moved to his side. "You could wash and cut the veg for the salad while I finish putting the crab cakes together. The bread for croutons is also cut and seasoned. It just needs to be placed in the oven."

"I can do that, but first," she had said while placing a hand at his waist to turn him to face her, "you'll tell me why you're being so Finn 1.0 from our first meeting instead of Finn 2.0 from yesterday and this afternoon."

She hadn't been about to endure another awkward minute and had been pleased when he'd finally met her eyes for more than a second. He hadn't answered, but he had slowly lifted his hands and settled them at her waist. His fingers had flexed as he'd slowly backed her against the counter—the same counter he'd had her on all those months ago. She'd placed her hands on his T-shirt-covered chest, smoothing her palms over the soft cotton and the hardened muscles beneath. "So," she had asked, "why do you not seem happy to be here?"

He'd closed the distance between their bodies, and Mirren had sighed as his hands had dragged up her sides to her back before his fingers had wrapped around her throat. His thumbs had tipped her chin up until their mouths had been close. She'd desperately wanted to sit on the counter again so that he could move between her thighs. She'd dreamed of his heat.

He had touched his lips once, then twice to hers. No tongue, chaste, simple. She had stood on tiptoe to get closer, an invitation to take it deeper, harder. He hadn't. Frustrating. "Finn," she'd begged.

"I am happy to be here. I never want to be anywhere else but by your side. It's just," he had begun, clearing his throat, "I thought about what I said to you and thought maybe I came on too strong. I was nervous coming tonight because I convinced myself you would pull back from me."

He'd wanted to be chatty at a moment when she'd wanted something altogether different from his mouth. "Does it look like I'm pulling back?"

"No, thank Christ, but..."

"But?"

"Are you still going to date other people?" He had cursed before placing another soft kiss. On her neck that time. "I knew

I wouldn't be able to wait five minutes to ask. I don't want to ruin our evening, but I also can't not know, damn it."

In that regard, she had relented to his overbearing ways. She would have been furious if he had seen someone else while they'd been apart. "I've been dating Brandon for a few months. I—"

"Exactly how long?" he'd interrupted.

"Four months." That admission had had his jaw flexing.

She'd given in to temptation and scratched her nails against his chiseled cheeks and dragged them through his beard. "Would it help if I told you we haven't gone further than kissing?"

"Tremendously," he'd admitted.

"I told him from the start that I wasn't over someone. He's been patient." She'd shrugged. "Brandon just never was...you."

"Thank fuck." He had taken her hands and brought her palms to his mouth, kissing each before holding them to his chest. "Just so we're clear, you won't see him again?"

"One more time. I asked him to meet me for a drink tomorrow after work. He deserves for me to at least break up with him in person."

"I'll come."

"You certainly will not." When he had opened his mouth to argue, she'd quickly said, "Kiss me."

Finn had taken a quick step back, putting his hands up as if to stop her from throwing herself at him. "What the hell is wrong with you? We've kissed before, if you'll remember."

The flighty bastard had had the nerve to smirk. "Oh, I remember, Mirren."

"Then—"

"I asked for dinner, a commitment, and a goodnight kiss. I'll be getting all three and in that order. I'm about proving you can trust me to keep my word."

He had gone back to his ingredients, his mood much brighter than it had been. Unfortunately, his good mood had left her body feeling achy and irritated.

Dinner had been wonderful. Finn really was good at cooking. Committing to being his exclusively had been an easy ask for Mirren to agree to. She'd already been his for those past several months. She just hadn't let herself admit it.

When she'd walked Finn to the door, it had been close to nine, and she hadn't been nearly ready for him to leave. During the evening, he'd touched her hair or hand or leg and given her chaste kisses. Basically, giving her what her heart wanted. Her body...not so much. It had wanted nails, teeth, and tongues. It had wanted a whole lot more than chaste.

Mirren had leaned against the door before he could reach for the handle, more than ready for her goodnight kiss. When he'd moved close and placed his hands flat on the door above her head, she hadn't been able to help the whimper that had escaped her throat.

"You want me, lass?" he had asked as his head had lowered to her mouth.

"You know I do."

"I know you're breaking things off with that idiot you've been seeing, but—"

"Brandon isn't an idiot. He just isn't..."

"Me."

Meet Confident Campbell, everyone. "He isn't you," she'd conceded.

"You've said you're ending it, and I trust that you will, but" —he had leaned close and licked her bottom lip, causing her breath to hitch and her core to spark—"will you commit to...just me? Only me?"

She would have committed to joining a bug-eating cult if it would have gotten his tongue down her throat. "Yes. Only you,

Finn." She hadn't even recognized her sex kitten voice and had ignored that her legs were trying to climb his body.

She.

Had.

Been.

Desperate.

Her declaration had been the feather that tipped the scale. Finn had had her lifted and her legs wrapped around his hips in a breath. *Finally, thank you, God, finally.* Their chests had aligned, and his mouth had taken hers in a desperate, wet, teeth-scraping, tongue-sucking kiss.

He'd had them so tightly wound together she hadn't been able to tell one pounding heartbeat from another. Finn had tangled his fingers in her hair. The pleasure and pain of the tugs had made her frantic. Impatient.

She'd had no breath for words like "more," "harder," "faster," but his body had seemed to know. His erection had been thick and hard behind his zipper, the metal teeth between them deliciously grating. She'd rotated her hips faster and faster, chasing the orgasm that had been threatening since the moment her feet had left the floor.

"Finn!" she'd panted, breaking the kiss long enough to nip his lower lip before delving her tongue roughly back inside his mouth. She had swallowed his moan and chased it with one of her own.

"Christ, Mirren," Finn had gritted out. "Come for me, baby. I want to see your face when I make you come."

Without losing her mouth, Finn had wedged a hand between their bodies, setting his palm over her center to increase the pressure until...

"Yes! God, yes! Don't move your hand!" Her body had writhed and bucked into his palm, her head arched back, neck straining, a keening moan falling from her open mouth.

Finn had trailed kisses up and down her neck, pinching her nipples. Another orgasm had been building behind the first from the way he'd worked her body. She'd been frantic to feel his weight above her, his sex breaching her until there was no ending or beginning between them.

The gallery's front door chimed, startling Mirren out of her memory. "Damn." Sighing at the ache between her legs—an ache she planned to have Finn remedy the moment she got home—she got up and straightened her clothes, preparing to greet the new security.

Mirren's legs wobbled slightly as she walked out of her office, her softer bits still pulsing from reliving Finn's goodnight "kiss." As she approached the front, she saw it wasn't the new security.

Lance Merte, the nosy boor of a reporter, was standing in the gallery proper, looking ill at ease.

"Lance. How have you been?" she asked without an ounce of enthusiasm. He looked like he hadn't slept in days and had what looked like a coffee stain on his collar. Nothing like his normal, polished self.

"Has anything...happened to Smith's artists? The twins?"

25

———

The moment Mirren had called him and asked him to come over, he'd left his sister and Lyle—who couldn't seem to keep their hands off each other—to jog the few blocks separating their houses. It had been a blessing to remove himself from his sister's sighs and blushes.

Finn was tense as he neared Mirren's. She had definitely sounded stressed on the phone. If that fucking Brandon had laid into her for breaking up with him, Finn would break his face.

The niggling voice that had been pestering him all day reared its ugly head again too. What if she'd changed her mind? Maybe she was about to deliver *his* face-to-face breakup.

Mirren must have seen him on one of the numerous security cameras her father had installed because the moment his foot landed on the first front doorstep, she was pulling the door open.

"Finn, thank you for coming."

Finn could see the stress wrapping its ugly fingers around Mirren as soon as he walked into her house. Stiff shoulders, pressed lips, and that was definitely worry in her eyes. "I always will, and I don't need to be thanked for it," he said gruffly, not liking the worry shadowing her lovely face, which made his own heart thunder. He took her hand as they walked into the kitchen. She didn't pull away, which surely she would have if things were over. "Tell me what's happened. Brandon?"

She huffed a laugh as she grabbed a bottle of Glenmorangie 18 and two glasses, setting them on the bar counter.

"Whisky before tea. The news must be dire," he said, trying for levity. Her lips barely twitched. *Sonofabitch.* Not good.

"I'm sorry for the dramatics. Jesus," she said, shaking her head, "I've had a hell of a day, and I'm about to make your day less pleasant, I'm afraid."

"Whatever it is, we'll work it out." And they would. If she tried to break up with him, he'd change her mind. He took the bottle of whisky from her hands and encouraged her to sit while he poured them two fingers each.

Mirren took a healthy sip, sighed, and sat back in her chair. "I needed that."

"Did you not have a drink when you met...Brandon?" He wanted to call him anything but his Christian name but refrained. He hadn't met the pansy, but no matter how many quality "attributes" the man had, he was still a poacher.

She met his eyes and raised her brows, not impressed with his not-so-subtle prying. "I did have a drink, but I didn't finish it. Drinking seemed a bit too celebratory for a breakup."

Christ, Finn hated the reminder that she had been involved enough with a man to even need a breakup. "How did he take it?"

"Not well."

"How not well?"

She rubbed her temples like she had a headache. Another reason to hate Brandon. "He was furious. He said I'd been leading him on. That I used him. He was right in a way. I had hoped I could move on, but I always knew you and I had unfinished business. We just... You and I, that is, we just seemed... You are the type of man I always wanted—that I knew I needed to be happy. I shouldn't have gone out with Brandon."

Mirren was being too hard on herself, though he was enough of a selfish bastard to admit that he loved that she hadn't been able to get over him. "I left you," he reminded her. "I hurt you. Could I change what I did, I assure you, I would. As for Brandon, good riddance. Now, go put some comfy clothes on while I make you a snack."

"Not yet." She shook her head, visibly still tense.

"What else, then? Just tell me."

"Lance Merte came by the gallery before close."

Finn tensed. "And why did that piece of shit darken your door? You've not spoken to him since the one date." It wasn't a question. Finn knew that Mirren had barely tolerated the reporter for the few hours she'd had to endure that evening at Alex and Sadie's pizzeria.

"Of course not. The man is beyond annoying, but tonight, I don't know, he seemed ... 'panicked' isn't the right word, but he was certainly stressed."

"Was he trying to get information about Fi and me?"

"Only to ask if anything had happened to the 'Smith Gallery artists,' which was weird enough, but then he added, 'the twins.' He knows who the Smiths are debuting, which is not surprising this close to the show and given the recent press releases. Everyone knows your names and little else, but...I don't know, Finn. Something was off.

"It was like he was worried. Why though? Why would he ask? Why would he care? I immediately called Lillias the moment he left. She and her brother have a vested interest in you guys and need to be aware that something might be going on. Though I felt all Dr. Who about bothering them."

Finn felt his heart stutter a few beats and took a sip of

whisky, giving himself a moment to think. "I know he was trying to get information about the museum's contestants, but I don't understand why he would ask you if anything had 'happened' to us. What the fuck is that about, Mir?"

"Exactly. It doesn't make sense. I wish I had something, anything, more to tell you. If he dug up something on your family, why come and ask me about it? He was...Christ, I don't know, scared almost."

Finn wasn't sure what to think. "Worst case scenario, Lance found out about"—he hesitated, not used to speaking about the past—"what our father did, and God forbid, he's planning on leaking the information to the artist community so that the judges find out. How would Fi's abuse affect her career? And, worse, her as a person?"

"It wouldn't. At least not for anyone remotely human. It would hurt your sister emotionally, but she's proven she's strong. She also has a larger support group than she ever had before."

Finn took a moment to gather his thoughts. "But, if it had been revealed before my sister decided to trust you and Lyle with her story, she would have withdrawn from the competition. She would have run. Not now, but she would have before."

Mirren's eyes widened. "Jesus, you're right. I haven't heard even a whisper about Fiona, and I assure you the Smiths would have been the first to hear even the slightest murmur. They would have told me."

"You told me once that Lance has a sister who's an artist and that maybe the date he took you on was a fact-finding mission. Surely, Lance or his sister isn't behind some of the shit that your Mr. Tall told you about."

"I can't imagine it, or I couldn't have, but after Lance's visit..."—she shrugged—"we can't rule it out. His sister, Hannah, was given an invitation to your event. Her mother is from a prominent family, and her patron gallery owner is good friends with Kain Smith. I can't imagine she means to cause trouble. It would do nothing more than sour the judges' opinions of Hannah, not Fiona."

"My sister won't withdraw from the competition, but I worry this will set her back even though she is determined to take a path of healing. She always said she was, but this is the first time I've believed her."

Mirren put her arms on the table, encircling their glasses to take his hands. "I believe in your sister. She's strong, intelligent, resilient, and extremely talented. If there is a storm, she'll weather it. We'll all weather it."

Mirren's support meant the world to Finn. She meant the world. "She can and will. You're right, and as much as I hate to admit it, I trust Lyle to have her back even though he's the handsiest motherfucker I've met."

She snorted in amusement. "Save me from overprotective men." Taking another sip of whisky, she continued to assure him. "Your art will be under real security tomorrow afternoon, but for now, you and Fiona need to take every precaution with yourselves as well. I would feel better if you called Lyle and explained the situation. Knowing him, the cameras are already up and running. Nothing will get by him. He'll also make sure your sister is prepared for anything that might be coming her way. I pray that isn't the case, but I admit, I've been unsettled since I spoke to Lance."

Mirren was doing her damnedest to make sure he and Fi were taken care of, so he called Lyle because it would put her mind at ease. Finn could admit that the man was capable. Lyle was steady. Exactly what his sister needed.

After Finn explained the situation, Lyle assured him that the security was covered and he could rest easy where Fiona was concerned. Strangely enough, after years and years of worrying, he hadn't felt that at ease since he was a child.

He insisted that Mirren go change. He wanted to take care of her like she always took care of everyone else. By the time she reentered the kitchen in comfy sweats and an oversized T-shirt, he'd just finished plating turkey sandwich triangles on toasted bread with homemade pimento cheese—which he'd slipped in his pocket before leaving his house—honey mustard, and pickles. A feast to complement Glenmorangie 18's rich flavors of spice, caramel, orange, and honey.

He arranged the fare within easy reaching distance from where she was seated before saying, "So far, we've spoken of two of your exes and my sister. Do you think there's a chance we might redirect the evening's conversation to things a bit more personal?"

Mirren gave him a serious look. "How personal?"

"How soon will you let me get you naked and take you to bed?"

MIRREN FELT her cheeks flush the moment Finn said the words "naked" and "bed." When she met his eyes, there wasn't a glimmer of amusement. He wasn't messing around, not that he normally did, but he *was* capable of being funny.

He wanted her, and she would have been a million times a liar if she said she didn't want him just as much.

"You could have had me last night." Mirren raised her brows in question. He'd left her in a melted puddle by the front door.

"I promised dinner, getting you to commit to me, and a goodnight kiss. I'm a man of my word."

Mirren barely stopped herself from snorting at what he considered a goodnight kiss. "And I'm hungry, and these sandwiches look divine. I love pimento," she tacked on, teasing him.

"They'll make a perfect snack after I have my way with you for a few hours."

When she didn't answer right away, he went on. "I thought when you called me tonight that you were going to tell me you'd changed your mind—that you thought Brandon was a better man than me. For you."

"Not possible."

He gave her a small nod of acknowledgement. "I'm an artist. I see my pieces swirling around me. They're in the air, on a blank wall, on the floor's tile. I see the creation of a piece, and my hands burn until I let them wield what my mind's eye has conjured.

"From the moment I walked into Smith Gallery and saw my Raven around your neck...you were mine. You always made me want things I didn't feel I had a right to want because of my sister. I'm free of my past chains now, and I warn you, Mirren MacGregor, I'm a decisive man. You are it for me. I've been burning to touch you again for months. If you could have seen my dreams"—he shook his head—"you would know thirst and want and need."

For a man of few words, Finn overwhelmed her with his confession. She decided that action would serve her at that moment. Finn needed reassurance that she didn't want any other man but him, and she would give it to him. She slid off her chair and, without asking permission, straddled his hips until they were face to face.

He gripped her hips and brought their lower bodies flush. It was an intimacy she'd felt only a few times before. Her core was already throbbing with want, remembering how he had felt against her the previous night. Mirren didn't want that time to be fast and furious, a firework flash that was over in a moment.

Finn wasn't the only one who'd dreamed of them together, of him between her thighs, arched over her body, his tongue dancing over every bit of her skin. She wasn't an artist, but she had a damn good imagination, and his body was a wonder to her. She felt his muscles flexing and shifting under her fingertips.

She leaned forward, and Finn mimicked her. "Do you think you're the only one who has suffered these past months? I've imagined you this way and in a million other positions."

She took her time, running her fingers alongside his neck and over his shoulders, flattening her palms against his chest. "Take your shirt off, Finn." He complied, and the smooth, unfettered expanse of skin burned her fingertips.

Mirren leaned back to allow herself access to his abdominals. The pads of her fingers slowly bumped over each ridge until they hit the waistband of his jeans. He sucked in a breath when her knuckles traced the barrier before tracking the deep V-lines that bracketed his stomach. She didn't go near the straining hard length between his legs. Not yet.

It was his mouth she wanted first. She slid her hands back over his shoulders until she could knead the muscles of his upper back, leaning in to gently brush his mouth once, twice, until on the third, she traced the seam of his lips with her tongue.

He opened his mouth with a groan, his tongue dipping deep the moment she opened hers. "Christ, Mirren. I could kiss you for weeks and never want to stop."

It stayed slow, a sharing of lips and breaths, whimpers and moans. She angled her head, letting him know she was ready for deeper and harder.

Breaking the kiss, he asked, "How many times did you touch yourself these past months? How many times did you come with my name in your mouth?" He gripped her chin until they were eye to eye.

"Too many to remember," she panted, trying to catch his

mouth again. When he kept holding her back, she admitted, "I used my fingers with my eyes closed, pretending it was your hand between my legs, pumping in and out, playing my body exactly the way I like. In bed, in the shower, and once...once at work."

"Fuck, baby." He finally took her mouth while unbuttoning her blouse and slipping it down her arms before unhooking her bra and flinging it to the table. Never breaking the kiss, he took advantage of her bared breasts, palming the firm globes and driving her crazy by pinching her peaked nipples and tugging the tips until her body was quivering.

Taking things slow was a memory. Their present was frantic —teeth and nails and moans—taking, giving, devouring. Her nails anchored in his back gave her a purchase to keep him right where she wanted.

His hands left her breasts, exchanging them for her hips, moving her in a back-and-forth rhythm, encouraging her to rock over his sex. She was so close to exploding, and he hadn't even taken her pants off.

Without warning, Finn broke their kiss and slid her hips down his thighs, putting distance between them. "I'm going to come in my pants if we keep going."

Taking a deep, shuddering breath, she admitted, "You aren't the only one."

"Tell me to take you to bed."

"Take me to bed."

They practically ran to her bedroom. The door was wide open. The moment their feet cleared the threshold, clothes were unbuttoned, unzipped, and discarded.

Mirren was naked. Finn was naked. All six feet, from toes to head, were a feast to behold. She knew his chest and back were sculpted works of art, but his legs were all long, lean, contracting muscles too. She'd only thought her imagination was worthy.

She looked him up and down, but her eyes refused to stray long from his...*Jesus*. "That... Your, umm...your dick is, ahh... bigger than I thought."

Finn chuckled before grasping his length and pumping slowly twice. "You've had your hands on me before, lass."

It was unfairly mesmerizing to see him touch himself. She shifted her legs. The burn he'd started between them in the kitchen was back and demanding.

"I must have been distracted," she answered, finally tearing her eyes from the show. "Plus, it's been months and months. I could have dreamed it all different shapes and sizes by now." Shrugging, she took a step toward him. Her voice might have been teasing, but her body was nothing but seriously focused.

26

Finn felt his lips curl up at her teasing. "Well, you can see for yourself," he said, dropping his hand to give her a full view. "You needn't strain your memory, lass." He loved the pink that stained her cheeks and the slight crease between her breasts and up her neck.

Christ, but she was stunning. While she'd been checking out his body, he'd been studying hers. He'd seen only bits and pieces of her body before that moment, but to see her then, all white and pink... He wanted to taste and touch every part. He had months of Mirren fantasies to make a reality.

Where would he begin? "Are we done with the looking phase, Miss MacGregor?"

"I was done with that months ago, Mr. Campbell. I'm past done—just waiting for you to catch up."

Cheeky Mirren was his favorite Mirren. She was ready. He was more than ready. Two strides, and he had her in his arms. Her gasp of surprised delight made him feel the lothario for the first time in his thirty years.

He settled her ass on the edge of the bed, and with one more desperate kiss, Finn placed his spread hand across her chest and gently pushed her slight form back until her frame was cushioned by the bed's pillow top.

She tried to wrap her legs around his hips, but he caught her knees, stopping her momentum. He took a deep breath as he looked down at Mirren, at the woman who had haunted his every thought for months, spread naked and exposed beneath him.

"You're in charge at the gallery, lass. Here, in this room, in this bed, it's my rules." He watched her eyes widen before narrowing. She clearly wasn't sure about giving him autonomy in the bedroom.

"Your rules?"

"Mine." And before she could question him more, he widened her knees until they touched the mattress, opening her bare sex to his gaze. Her mouth snapped shut. He felt a slight pressure against his palms, where she was testing his strength.

He met her curious stare and kept it while he leaned forward. "Finn." The way she said his name, all breathless with need, made him even harder, drawing the sensitive skin surrounding his balls impossibly tight. His body was screaming at him to sink into her willing body, but he wouldn't find release until he'd discovered what Mirren MacGregor tasted like.

Her ass began to squirm, so he let her knees go and brought his firm grip to her inner thighs to arrest any movement she might attempt. He allowed his thumbs to brush the sides of her open slit. She closed her eyes and moaned, straining against his touch.

"Look at me, Mirren." Her eyes blinked lazily open. "You want my mouth on you? Have you ever had a man's tongue here?" he asked before blowing warm breath over her sensitive folds.

"Please," she begged, raising her ass off the bed, trying to close the gap between his mouth and her center. Her fists were white knuckled as they held the bed's covers above her head.

"Have you?" He shouldn't have needed to know, but he couldn't help the inner caveman riding his possessive self.

"Christ, Finn, no! And you won't be the first if you don't stop teasing me, you ass!"

"First, last, and only," he corrected. He loved her temper. Hell, he loved her if he were being honest, though thankfully, he wasn't so far gone that he didn't know it was too soon to admit such a thing.

He'd made them both wait long enough, and without another word, he made his first long, deep foray into her sex, which instantly made beads of precum leak from the head of his sex, wetting his stomach.

Mirren was uninhibited in her pleasure. Her cries and pants were a symphony. Her hands holding his head firmly to her body were insistent.

"Your taste, Christ," he cursed, his last coherent word before wringing two screaming orgasms from her body.

He kissed his way up her stomach, sucking roughly on each of her pricked nipples while pushing her body toward the center of the big bed, where he could finally, finally, cover her body with his.

She looked near to passing out, so he chided her quietly while kissing her eyes, jaw, and ears. "No sleeping yet, lass. I'm not nearly done with you." Her soft sigh and smile made him take her mouth in a tender kiss.

"Are you ready?" She wasn't a novice to passion and certainly not to self-pleasure, as she'd readily admitted... Still... "For me," he added the ridiculously juvenile explanation. He'd just made the woman beneath him scream his name, and here he was blushing like a boy and not a man of at least moderate experience.

She surprised him by lightly running her fingers over his back and shoulders, his neck, and then his lips. "I'm boneless, sated, and perhaps leaning more toward catatonic than bright eyed, but oh, yes, I'm so, so ready. You've made me so ready, Finn," she added seriously.

Mirren backed up her words by raising her knees until her legs created a vee about his hips, bringing their sexes in alignment. "My God, lass, your heat will set me off." They simultaneously flexed into one another, and the resulting moans had him flexing every muscle in his body to stop himself from aligning himself and driving home.

Mirren wasn't half so reticent. She began rubbing her slickness up and down his shaft until the choice of slow or fast or soft or rough was taken from him.

Propping his upper body up with his elbows, he was able to match her pelvis roll for roll, and on the last roll, his engorged head breached fucking heaven on earth. "Mirren, God, Mirren," he choked as he slowly entered her for the first time.

"Kiss me, Finn, and finish what you've started," she demanded.

He did as the lady asked. He took her mouth and her body for hours—until there wasn't a millimeter of skin he hadn't tasted or touched.

When literature described sex as a religious experience, he agreed...applauded the depiction, in fact.

Finn ensured Mirren was sleeping soundly before he slipped from their bed, praying he could finish one more piece for the exhibition before she woke up.

He had started and discarded a sculpture months ago, thinking it didn't fit with his other exhibit pieces. Looking at Mirren MacGregor's peaceful face just then, he realized the unfinished work was the axis that all his art circled.

27

———

Hannah's Voices

"She's losing it."

"She needs to take better care of herself."

"Then stop pushing her down the stairs."

"Shut up! You made her bang her head on the wall yesterday until that unattractive lump completely ruined the back of her head. Now she'll have to hide it under some god-awful hat."

"If she didn't like the pain, she would end it."

"She needs to end it. I'm tired of being here. She's weak. Eventually, she'll snuff herself out."

"None of this is new."

"That's the problem! Nothing is ever new! The fat cow does nothing but bumble through her days."

"She isn't a cow. We don't let her eat enough for that."

"No one wants her to look like her ridiculous mother. Christ, that woman turns my stomach."

"Forget the mother. Look at what we have to deal with. She's all but curled in a ball on the floor."

"She's rocking herself like an infant."

"She's squeezing her head. As if that will keep us out."

"She'll never be picked for the museum exhibit."

"Never."

"She's pathetic. She has all of us helping her day in and day out, yet she's still helplessly pathetic."

"I hate her."

"I hate her more."

Mirren slowly came awake, her sore body making lovely complaints as her back arched and her hips thrust skyward in a glorious stretch for what felt like the hundredth time since consciousness had found her.

She and Finn had consumed each other's bodies for hours upon hours the night before, and the fun might not have been over. Her new lover was insatiable if the teeth nipping at her shoulder were an indicator of his continued interest.

"Finn," she huffed in amusement.

"Mirren," he answered in an even tone as he glided his fingers along her arm, tracing over her collarbone and down the other arm.

She shivered at how lovely that felt. "Mmm" was her response. Her eyes were still closed, not quite ready to commit to the morning.

She finally let her eyes flutter open and gasped as bright, slashing streams of sunlight blazing through the bedroom's shutters hit her in the face. "Christ, Finn. The movers will be at your place to load your and Fiona's pieces soon. You've made me derelict in my duty in a single night," she teased, continuing to stretch and enjoy his lips skating over her sensitive skin.

"Mmm, enough time for a shower, I should think" was his lazy answer.

Mirren's eyes finally adjusted as a completely dressed Finn straddled her naked hips. "Hey," she exclaimed, "why are you dressed?"

"I had a last-minute piece to finish."

His avoidance of eye contact had her more than curious. "Did you? So, you left me to sleep on my own?" Another thought hit her. "Did you even sleep?"

"No, and I'm more than happy with the trade." He smirked.

Curiouser and curiouser.

"Did you mention a shower?" she asked wistfully. "I imagine there isn't a part of my body that couldn't do with a good bit of hot water and soap."

"I could wash your bits with my tongue," he offered, a serious expression in place.

"You're impossible, Mr. Campbell. If we go down that path, your art will stay behind cupboard doors instead of in the gallery," she chided, though his suggestion had her briefly arching her hips toward his.

"Shower, then breakfast. I've already started the coffee, so best you hurry," he announced before sweetly kissing her lips.

With a much higher level of athleticism than she could lay claim to, Finn rolled off her body and the bed, extending a hand to pull her to her feet, like a gentleman. He led her like a lamb to the shower while she tried valiantly to contain a girlish squeal of delight. A grin kept popping out, but that simply couldn't have been helped. The man she'd been obsessed with for months was holding her hand. In her bedroom. If there were a reincarnated goddess of all things surreal, surely, Mirren would be her embodiment.

And she wasn't a virgin anymore. That crazy bit of news kept running through her mind, especially as the soreness between her legs proved she and Finn had done work the previous night.

Mirren leaned against the cool marble of the bathroom counter, watching Finn fiddle with the shower knobs and heads. Steam started to build up on the sides of the clear glass.

When he turned and saw her casual pose, he walked to her and picked her up, setting her bare ass on the cold counter. She squeaked in surprise. "Brr! My butt likes things a bit warmer."

"We'll both warm up soon enough." He bent to kiss her mouth before moving to her neck and chest, leaving no bits untouched as he leisurely explored.

She should have reminded him again of the busy morning that lay ahead, but she buried her face in the crease of his neck and breathed deeply instead. "Mmm. You smell like your workshop."

He grasped the back of her head and bent her neck back enough so that she could see his smile. "Do I?" he asked. "And what does that smell like?"

"Metal, earth, and fire. They happen to be three of my favorite scents since I met you." Mirren wasn't lying. Finn's craft smelled powerful, and she was woman enough to admit that that was exactly how she liked her men. No wonder Brandon had never done it for her.

She watched as he divested himself of his T-shirt, boots, socks, jeans, and underwear. Her cold ass was forgotten. "Jesus, you're lovely to look at." His answering grin had her sliding from the counter and purposefully letting her side brush his newly freed and already bobbing erection as she made her way to the open end of the shower, knowing he would follow.

She tugged the hairband from her wrist to create a messy bun, high enough that the ends of her hair wouldn't get wet.

Finn picked up a bar of exfoliating oatmeal soap that River O'Faolain had sent her and sniffed it.

"Wet your hair and beard and then sit on the bench"—she pointed behind him at the smooth stone shelf she used to shave her legs or relax on in the shower's heat—"and let me wash it for you." His surprised look was comical. For him, showers were probably done out of necessity and finished with efficiency.

While he stood under the heavy spray, the bigger jets tapping against his flexing muscles and the softer spray wetting his hair, she picked up a lovely bottle of oatmeal honey shampoo —also from River—and poured out a generous dollop into her palm.

Once he sat, she asked him to turn sideways on the bench. "Lean your head back against my chest so I can give you a scalp massage."

"This seems decadent," he grumbled while complying.

Bending to smack a kiss to his lips, she teased, "Sex isn't the only perk to having a partner."

"Clearly. Have at me, lass." He grinned, leaning back enough for her to catch his wink.

As she worked to lather his hair and beard, she massaged his scalp, jaw, and neck until he was softly moaning. "Nice?"

"Nice? Christ, Mir, any nicer, and I'll melt into the tiles at your feet."

"Now rinse because we really do need to get a move on." He grabbed her hand as he stood and took her with him to stand under the spray. She picked up a washcloth and swiped the soft bar of soap across the cotton several times before scrubbing her body.

Finn mimicked her routine. The moment the last of the suds slid from their bodies, he bent to take her mouth in a hot, open-mouthed kiss that quickly got out of control. Spinning her around, he put her back against the warm, slick tiles, using them as leverage. While he continued to ravage her mouth, their hands explored.

She stroked the hard length against her stomach, arching her head back until the kiss broke and she could see Finn's intense expression leaning over her. "I want this"—she stroked him, squeezing the head firmly before backtracking his length—"in my mouth."

His hips bucked against her body. "Fuck me," he groaned.

"That's the plan." She had started to sink to her knees when he caught her shoulders, suspending the motion.

"Rain check," he growled. "If we only have a small window of time, I want to spend it inside you." Gripping her ass with his long fingers, he pulled her up. "Wrap your legs around me, Mir. I need you. Now."

Before her ankles had even hooked, his sex was sliding past her slickened folds. "Finn," she moaned, able to do nothing but take whatever he gave her. He hammered into her, hitting that perfect spot over and over and over again.

She felt the telltale rush of tingles through her core until she tightened around him, pulsing and pulling him deeper. She could only chant, "Finn, Finn, Finn, Finn."

A stream of guttural grunts left his throat, along with a string of nonsense words and curses. "Mirren, stay... Can't... God, there... Yes, Christ... Tight... Coming... Yes... *Fuck yes!*"

She felt him kick and pulse deep inside as she clung helplessly to his stiff shoulders and willed her intense aftershocks to cease so her uncontrollable whimpers might as well.

"I'd set you down, lass, but I fear my hands might be permanently glued to your gorgeous ass." He dropped his forehead to her shoulder, taking deep gulps of air. Their chests touching, hearts pounding a synced rhythm.

Mirren was about to reply when, through the bits of steam-free glass, she thought she saw movement. Alarm started to fill her body when she tipped her head to the side to look out a particularly clear bit of glass to see...

"Oh my God," she breathed. Finn must have heard the panic in her voice and was in the process of pulling out to let her down. "No! Christ, no. Don't move," she whispered in his ear. "We have an audience."

He followed her line of sight and turned to stone. "Mir?"

Clearing her throat of mortification, she addressed the three sets of wide eyes staring back at her. "Hello, girls," she started in an excessively loud and perky voice, signing for Blair's sake—at an awkward angle while attempting to keep her breasts glued to Finn's chest.

Three little girls, ages three to four years, were looking way too curious for comfort. The audience included her sister Gray, with her long honey-blond hair; her other sister, Mags, sporting precious black ringlets; and her wee cousin Blair, with her wild red curls—the threesome looked like dolls...ornery dolls.

Talking over the sound of the water, which she dared not turn off to let the steam dissipate further, she asked, "Are your mamas downstairs?" *Please, God, let it just be their mothers.*

Sassy Mags answered. She may have looked like their father, Charles, with her black hair and straight, aristocratic nose, but her personality, unfortunately, was all her big sister's. Mags was a miniature Mirren. "Nah. This is a daddy-daughter trip. All the daddies are downstairs waiting to see you."

Gray spoke next. "Don't worry, Sister, I folded your shirt and his"—she nodded toward Finn—"and I even picked your bra off the table. You're messy. Momma makes me put my dirty clothes in the hamper."

"Yeah, she tried to hide your bra from the men," Mags added, "but Uncle Colly saw and took it." Mirren heard Finn's muttered "Christ." "Daddy thought it was funny."

"Daddy" *would* have found that situation amusing. She

could always count on her Morrow dad to find her MacGregor dad's and her uncle Coll's overprotective natures funny. The dread of what was awaiting her below was giving her an upset stomach.

Poor Finn's face was frozen in horror. Ignoring that they were still naked and her legs were still wrapped around his hips, she attempted to get the girls to move along. Signing and speaking together, she said, "Okay, girls, why don't you go see if there's anything for breakfast."

"We stopped at a restaurant and picked up tons of food. Mommy tried calling you bunches of times last night when Daddy decided to surprise you. She said your phone was dead." Gray looked disgusted as she spoke, as if she couldn't imagine being so irresponsible. *Humbling.*

"The moms are having a mommy-daughter day with the grandmas and the babies." Mags rolled her eyes at the mention of Blair and Gray's new brothers, Laith and Lachlann. "They're all coming in a few days for your show, Mir Mir."

Mirren swallowed her groan of frustration, but she would have sworn on a Bible that the men in her family were mind-reading warlocks. Somehow, the ogres knew she'd had sex the night before and wanted to block any more such endeavors.

Blair signed, "Sleepover," and clapped her hands.

Finn melted Mirren's heart when he told her to "Hang on" so he could have use of his hands and then wiped a larger portion of steam far from their upper bodies away before signing and saying out loud, "I'll bake everyone's favorite cookies. I love to bake cookies."

Blair, Mags, and Gray squealed their excitement, grinning widely at one another like they'd never heard anything so amazing.

Mirren whispered for Finn's ears only, "It's really hard to be mad at all that cuteness."

He gently pinched her side before sighing and whispering, "It is, but, Mir, for the love of all that's holy, please get rid of the audience before softened parts of my anatomy decide to slip from a part of yours."

She almost giggled at his martyred tone. "Okay, girls, head on downstairs while Mr. Campbell and I get dressed."

Mags, of course, asked, "Why are you bathing with a boy? I take baths all the time with Gray and Blair, but he's a *boy*."

Lord, have mercy, Mirren silently prayed. "Sometimes, adults like to save money by showering together to use less water." She knew as soon as the explanation was out of her mouth that it was a mistake.

Mags grabbed her sister's and cousin's hands. "Let's go ask our dads if they shower with our mommies."

The mischievous twinkle in the little girl's eyes didn't bode well. *Was she that big of a shit growing up?* Most definitely yes.

The three bringers of mayhem filed out, leaving Mirren and Finn naked and, thankfully, finally, alone. He slowly lowered her feet to the floor. They both hissed a bit as their sensitive parts slid free of one another. He may not have been hard anymore, but there was still enough of him inside to make her wish they had time for another go.

"If you keep eyeing my dick that way, lass, we're really going to get ourselves in trouble with your menfolk."

He chuckled when she glared at him and shut off the water. "As if we didn't have enough to do today for the show. Now we have to deal with...them. Oh, God, Finn. I bet you didn't expect to have to deal with my family circus just because you slept with me."

Mirren felt her cheeks heat as she grabbed two towels and handed one to Finn. She was trying to laugh it off, but she really was mortified that not only did her dads and uncle know she'd had sex, but they would also believe themselves within their rights to question Finn.

Mirren watched him, fascinated to see all his muscles flexing while he briskly dried his body. His hair stood on end, all a dark, deep umber with highlights of carmine and wine and copper. Lovely.

He was dried and dressed within minutes. She, on the other hand, was wrapped in a towel and still applying lotion. He walked back into the bathroom and gave her a quick kiss.

"I'll see you downstairs. I'll let Fi know we'll be running behind and to start loading without us."

"Don't tell me you mean to greet that bunch alone, Finn. Surely, you aren't feeling suicidal."

He chuckled, for Christ's sake. "Not suicidal, but I am going down."

29

"Don't go down there without me, Finn. Christ, you'll be walking into a firing squad!" Mirren pleaded.

"I respect your family, lass, but I don't fear them." *Mostly true.* Her wide, panicked eyes said how foolish she thought he sounded. "I won't hide behind you and pretend that you aren't mine and I'm not yours." He brought one of her hands to his lips to kiss her inner wrist. "And I won't hide my feelings."

She sighed, but her eyes sparkled. Clearly, his admitting his feelings had put a good-sized dent in her misgivings. She admitted, "I won't hide mine either."

"I would have preferred to speak with your family before they found out that we're...intimate. And I really would have preferred not to give the little ones a show. Thank Christ hot water creates steam or the girls would have far more to tell their mothers about." He felt his neck heat with embarrassment at the thought.

"If you stick around this time, you'll get used to having a noisy big family butting into every moment of your life."

She chuckled, but Finn heard the slightest edge in her voice.

He stepped forward and took her hands, stilling them from pumping out more lotion.

"Mirren." Her head tipped back slightly at his serious tone. "I'm not going anywhere. Tell me you believe that."

She quickly started to say, "Of course," but he stopped her. "No, not 'of course.' We didn't just have sex, Mir. It was never just sex. We made commitments. We *both* made them, and I need to know that you believe I will honor mine." He gently tipped her chin up when her eyes dropped.

She looked sheepish. "I do believe you, damn it. I'm...damn, I guess I might be feeling a little emotional since it was my first time, and I...I care so much about you. It made me nervous that it might—"

"End," he finished for her. She dipped her chin against his fingers once, her cheeks turning pink. "Never." He cupped her jaw and placed a chaste kiss on her lips. A promise. "I'm not taking what we've done lightly.

"Now, tell me you believe I'm here for the now and the tomorrows. And, Christ, hurry up about it. Every second those three downstairs have to wait and wonder what I'm doing to their precious girl can only mean bad things for me."

Mirren laughed then, her face clearing and lighting up. "I believe you," she assured him with a grin. "Go on, then, but there better not be any fisticuffs. It's Dad and Uncle Coll's favorite way to settle disagreements. Plug my phone in on your way out, please. Had I not let the damn thing die, we wouldn't be in this mess."

"Don't blame yourself. You had your hands full with...bigger things."

Mirren choked on a giggle. "Take yourself and your dick jokes downstairs, Campbell."

Finn jogged down the stairs, hoping Mirren was only

teasing about what he would find, but one look at the two giant best friends and the dark-haired Charles Morrow waiting in the kitchen and scowling at his approach with crossed arms indicated violence might be a real possibility. MacGregor and Barr brought to mind the Gods of war and fire, Ares and Hephaestus. At least Mirren's other dad, Charles, smiled before shrugging and grimacing.

"Good morning."

Silence greeted him until Charles coughed and managed to get out, "Good morning, Mr. Campbell."

"Call me Finn, please, Mr. Morrow."

"Charles will do for me, then, and I'm very happy to meet you again. I never want to see my sweet Mirren hurt, so I'll trust you are as honorable as she believes."

Okay, then. No beating about the bush. "I am," Finn answered immediately. One down, two to go.

Deciding to ignore the statues continuing to watch him silently, Finn looked to the small breakfast table where the three girls were giggling and eating breakfast. Speaking aloud and signing for Blair, he asked, "I've oranges if you young ladies fancy a glass of juice." At their smiles and claps, Finn went to the cabinet over the sink and brought down Mirren's juicer.

"Know your way about my daughter's house, do you?"

The hairs on the back of Finn's neck rose at the threatening tone of Thomas MacGregor's low growl. Finn met the man's eyes, praying his nervousness didn't show. "I lived here with my sister. You'll remember?"

Thomas was about to make a remark when, surprisingly, Mirren's uncle, Coll, interrupted the tense standoff. His eyes softened when they briefly landed on his fiery-headed daughter giggling with her cousins. "My wee Cat is happy you can speak with our daughter." And then, as though the words were pulled kicking and screaming from his throat, Barr added, "I am thankful too."

Finn nodded at the man's admission, not feeling hopeful necessarily but at least appreciating that Coll had bent enough to thank him. However, he felt slightly uncomfortable discussing his BSL skills since he knew Barr was aware of why he'd learned them.

He started cutting oranges into halves. "Fiona is looking forward to seeing the young ones," he told the three men, cringing when he cleared his throat like a nervous Nancy.

"I looked at the camera feeds. You stayed here last night."

The barely restrained anger in MacGregor's voice had Finn's shoulders tensing, but he refused to allow Mir's dad to intimidate him. "I did." And then, because he wouldn't—no, couldn't—back down in front of that group, he foolishly added, "She's mine."

MacGregor was a blond blur as he rushed Finn, who quickly shut off the juicer. He'd told Mirren not thirty minutes ago that he wasn't afraid of her family, but Christ.

"Thomas," Coll warned at his best friend's shoulder.

MacGregor glanced at the table of children and took a shuddering deep breath. He lowered his voice so only Finn and the three other men could hear him. "The hell she is yours. She is mine...ours." He quickly looked at Charles and dipped his head in apology.

Finn was just about finished putting up with the man's bullshit and could only pray that if or when he became a father, he wouldn't be such an ass.

Ignoring MacGregor's comment for the moment, he grabbed three glasses and the pitcher of juice and went to serve the girls. He picked up the juicer on his way back and started rinsing the parts in the sink. "She is your daughter. I never said she wasn't, but Mirren and I are..." He paused, not sure how to explain their new relationship. He settled on "We are committed."

Her dad's jaw tensed, and Finn could tell MacGregor wanted to deny him again. He was shocked when the other man said, "I have known of Mirren's feelings, and I did encourage you and your sister to move back here. I didn't encourage you to begin a...well...to begin a relationship with my daughter that included spending the night."

Finn bit back the grin that wanted badly to break free. Big bad Thomas MacGregor was blushing. Out of the corner of his eye, he saw Mirren's other father spin around and pretend to be interested in something his daughter, Mags, was saying, but there was no hiding the man's shaking shoulders.

Charles Morrow had quite a sense of humor, and Coll Barr was more interested in watching over his daughter than in Finn. *Thank you, Jesus.* Thomas was a good father—an excellent father, the type of father he wished he and his sister had had, so he couldn't truly be angry over the man's gruff posturing.

Finn swallowed his pride because the man deserved respect. "I won't leave Mir again, but..."—he shook his head in bewilderment at what he was about to say—"I should have waited to... to...umm...slee—"

"Don't you dare say what I think you're about to, young man."

Finn coughed in disbelief. "Not so young, MacGregor. There's probably only ten years between us."

"Not a good argument, Campbell," Coll warned.

Finn was reaching the end of his patience with the confrontation. Still, he was determined to give Mirren's family respect. "I should have spoken to...her fathers before...before we...before..." *Kill me, God. Just strike me dead.*

Finn didn't realize Mirren had come into the kitchen until she spoke. "Okay, Dads and Uncle, your time to play Conan the Barbarian has come to an end, and just so you know, I've only just hung up with Mom, Jo, and Cat, who have been watching this whole meet and greet live thanks to me."

And they could have heard a pin drop.

30

They didn't think she could handle the pressure. They didn't think she could do what needed doing.

They were wrong.

She was strong. She wouldn't let anything or anyone stand in her way when it came to becoming a world-renowned artist.

This piece of drugged-out shit would never win.

The bastard's cut wrists, pumping his life's blood into the murky water of his dirty bath, proved she would be the only winner in the end.

Hannah stood and looked at herself in the cracked mirror. She was smiling, happy, as she pinched a bloody razor blade between her fingers.

She was a winner.

She would win.

Her grin widened until her teeth looked almost feral smiling back at her.

"Weak, am I?

"Pathetic?

"You want me to kill myself?

"I think you need to remember that if I die, you die."

She laughed as she lightly dragged the tip of the razor over the jugular veins of her neck, leaving a trail of red from the dirty blade on the sensitive skin before trailing the sharp edge between her breasts, over the scarred skin of her abdomen, and up the arterial lines of each wrist.

"I could end you as easily as I ended that pile of shit in the tub. Keep testing me.

"I dare you."

31

———

"**D**ad, Mom said she appreciates how kind you were to Finn, but you have to stop finding awkward family moments so hilarious. She also said she'll call you when she leaves Grandma and Grandpa's house. She sounded as miserable as expected, and she's only spent an hour with those... humorless cretins."

"They're the worst," Charles agreed before remembering that the "humorless cretins" were also Coll's parents. "No offense, Barr."

"None taken. I would call them worse than that, except Blair has become quite the lip reader."

Mirren had every man's attention, and Finn was about to pull a Charles and laugh at the look of horror on MacGregor's face.

Mirren continued, "Dad, Jo would like you to call her."

MacGregor looked surprised. "That's all?" he asked suspiciously.

"Hardly—if I know my stepmother as well as I think. I would like a moment of your time as well."

"For?"

"To discuss boundaries. Specifically security camera usage." When her dad grimaced, Mirren had mercy and hugged him tightly around his waist. "You raised me to be smarter than you're giving me credit for."

MacGregor gave Finn a "We aren't finished" look before hugging his daughter tight to his side and admitting, "You're right."

Patting her dad on the arm, like he were a child who'd answered correctly, she finished with her uncle. "And Colly, Aunt Cat was very happy with you."

Before Barr could puff his chest out, she added, "But she wants you to pay more attention to what your daughter says to her cousins."

Everyone looked at the table, and three identical, not-so-innocent grins met the adults' gazes. The little ones must have been following the conversation.

"Blair, would you tell Daddy what you've—"

Finn was startled, probably not more than her uncle, when Mirren interrupted. "I think you should discuss that with Blair later. I'm ready for breakfast."

Her wide smile looked forced, and the excitable clap of her hands was definitely off. She must have known what Blair had said and didn't want the child... And then it dawned on Finn. The moment "Oh shit" left his mouth, the young girls were deep in the throes of shrill giggles, and he realized too late what wee Blair was about to reveal.

Finn's eyes went wide, and his damnably fair skin surely scorched a brilliant red when he watched in silent horror as Blair signed to her father that "Finny has bits and bobs just like you, Daddy." *Fuck me two ways to Sunday.*

Coll's face turned scarlet before he quickly told his daughter, "Enough of that, Kitten." She stuck her lip out in a pout for all of two seconds before Mags hid her hands below the table and signed something clearly not meant for adult eyes, making Blair chuckle.

MacGregor went from decently moderate to berserker in a blink. His jaw clenched, and he was probably about to demand why Finn might have been found naked in his daughter's room—even though, at that point, he had to have known what was what—when his daughter interrupted.

"My daddy has bits and bobs too," Gray shared, which had MacGregor's face turning as red as Finn's—and surely saved Finn from another ass chewing.

"Well, my daddy does too," Mags said as she made a flourishing hand wave over her lap. "I'm glad I don't have all that stuff."

Gray rolled her eyes and crossed her arms over her chest. "Mommy says all of Daddy's bits are precious. Gross," she finished before sticking her tongue out at Mags.

Blair was happily sipping her orange juice, tapping her heels against the wooden legs of her chair. As the youngest, she was precocious but so lovey, it was no wonder Mirren's uncle melted with only a word from his daughter. That was proven a moment later when she signed, "I love you, Daddy."

"I love you too, Kitten."

Finn noticed there was no reservation in Barr's response. MacGregor, Barr, and Morrow were everything he wished his own father had been for himself but mostly for his sister.

"Okay, girls," Mirren interjected, shaking her head in exasperation, "I know very well you didn't see Finny's...anything, so you three can stop with the tall tales or I'll ring our moms." The girls' eyes went wide at the threat, and Finn shared a smirk with the other men. Who knew that something so ridiculously embarrassing could bring him closer to Mirren's family?

"Fine," the three said and signed simultaneously.

"But Finny was holding you," Gray had to add.

And the nail in the coffin... Mags added, "In the shower."

Mirren shook her head at Finn and lifted her hands in surrender. She was doing her damnedest to ignore the two men wearing thunderclouds and even Charles, who, as per normal, was biting his lip to keep from smiling.

Deciding the morning was past saving, Finn stepped forward, gaining a lot of unwanted male attention. He placed a lidded paper cup of coffee into Mirren's hand. "Best go help Fi with the movers."

Mirren latched onto her coffee cup like it was the answer to every whispered prayer. "Yes." She threw kisses to the girls and gave quick goodbyes to everyone else, practically dragging Finn out the front door.

MacGregor stopped their escape. "You'll meet us for lunch, Mir?" At his daughter's raised brow and unimpressed look, he cleared his throat and added, "With Fiona and Lyle, of course... and Campbell."

They'd almost cleared the threshold when they heard Charles tell MacGregor, "Don't forget your blood pressure medicine, mate. This much stress can't be good for you." His voice shook with barely stifled laughter.

"I'm not on blood pressure medicine, *Charles*," MacGregor growled, "and you'll remember that you are years older than I am."

Before Finn shut the door, they heard "Four, Thomas. Four."

Once outside, Mirren grabbed Finn's hand, dragged him to the side of the house, and kissed him and kept kissing him until his hands were clutching her ass to pull her close. She was sucking on his tongue and making satisfied little noises.

He had to swipe a small tree branch covered in leaves off his shoulder when their kiss found them leaning against the nearest sturdy tree trunk. "We have to stop, Mir. We can't go back to your room without starting a world war with your family, and I refuse to take you up against the rough bark of this tree, no matter how badly I want to be inside you again."

"There's a blind spot for the cameras right here. It's why I chose to drag you over here."

"As much as I appreciate not putting on a show for your fathers, I refuse to take any chances. I happen to like my balls right where they are."

"I know, I know. I just want to spend hours and days touching you and having you touch me," she replied honestly, smiling sheepishly. "I fear I'm coming off as incredibly young, but now that this thing has happened between us, I can't think about anything except when I can have you naked again, and my family showing up for a surprise visit is so annoying, and we still have to deal with the gallery thing!

"Okay"—she laughed—"your artwork is a lot more than a 'thing.' I'm just—"

"You like orgasms more than my jewelry."

"Well, maybe." She grinned before poking him in the stomach. "Though I'm never giving you your ravens back."

She'd shown him the full *Unkindness* the night before. It wasn't that he hadn't believed she truly had the entire collection, but he'd found it incredible that *she* had it. "They're exactly where they were meant to be." It sounded cheesy to his own ears, but that didn't make it less true. It had killed him a little to sell them, but look at where his ravens had led him.

She brushed the last of the leaves from his shoulders and led the way back to the front path where her car sat. They made the quick drive to his house, where Fiona and Lyle were already directing the movers packing up her paintings into the moving truck.

When Mirren went to speak to the movers, Finn walked to

his sister, sparing a brief glance Lyle's way, attempting to ignore the man's familiarity with Fiona's body. He mentally cursed himself. *Do you want to come off like MacGregor, mate?*

He kissed her cheek. "How's it going, Fi?" Her immediate grin made him grin back. She was truly happy.

"On schedule. That is the last of mine." She nodded toward two brown-paper-wrapped paintings leaning against the front gate.

"I worked on another piece last night, so I need to go box it."

"I had a notification from the alarm cameras that you were in your shop from one this morning until about an hour and a half ago." She raised her brows in question.

"I was inspired." Lyle was standing behind Fiona, smiling and winking, but thankfully, he kept his mouth shut.

"Oh, that's lovely. I can't wait to see it."

Before Finn could take his leave, he noticed Mirren was on the phone. Whatever was being discussed had put a pinched look on her face. He changed course and went to her side. He was pleased when she wrapped an arm around his waist.

"I understand, Lillias. Yes. I'll make sure of it." Mirren ended the call and motioned for Fiona and Lyle to join them.

"What's happened?" Finn asked.

"I just spoke to Lillias Smith. She informed me that an old family friend of theirs who lives on an estate near Aberdeen just rang up Kain. They had been secretly backing an artist for the competition—the Smiths didn't even know until this morning.

"The artist was just found in a rundown motel bathtub, dead with his wrists slit. Apparently, he'd been on a four-day bender, doing drugs and prostitutes to celebrate finishing his collection for the competition.

"Lillias said the police are investigating. They believe it might have been staged. That he didn't commit suicide. The

Aberdeen estate had an attempted break-in two nights ago, but the alarm scared off whoever made the attempt.

"If it wasn't suicide, if someone actually killed him, that person might have tried to get to his paintings first.

"He painted with oil," Mirren finished grimly.

32

———

Mirren felt the black coffee she'd drunk on her way to Finn's hit her empty stomach like a charred stone. Fiona and Finn looked bewildered. Lyle was already on the phone, presumably with her uncle Coll or her dad.

Had she not been so taken aback by Lillias's call, she would have thought to make the call herself. "Is that Coll?" she asked Lyle. At his nod, she told him to put her uncle on speaker. "I would like you to look into Lance Merte. He's an investigative reporter. Also, Hannah Todd, Lance's sister. She's an artist."

She quickly related her few encounters with Lance and went over Mr. Tall's information too. Finn stood behind her and placed supporting hands on her shoulders. "They might have absolutely nothing to do with this, but I have a bad feeling, Uncle Coll, especially with how strange Lance was acting last night."

Mirren heard a muffled conversation that sounded suspiciously like an argument. Her dad had entered the conversation. Lyle gave her a tight smile and a shrug.

Her dad must have taken Coll's phone because his deep voice came on. "Why didn't you call me last night?"

She wasn't about to tell him that Finn had distracted her. "I'm sorry, Dad. I should have. I thought it was strange, but it wasn't until Lillias called me just now about the artist in Aberdeen that my concern escalated. The Smith Gallery event is tomorrow night. Hopefully, nothing else happens."

"You should have called me last night."

Christ. "Dad."

"You are to go nowhere alone until this mess is cleared up."

Mirren knew from past experience that her dad would not be moved by any argument, so she answered with a simple "Understood."

"Coll is taking Sloan and May off another case. They are excellent at blending in and lethal as hell. They will guard the Campbells and you. Lyle is going with Fiona to the exhibition, I assume."

"I am," Lyle confirmed.

"Get Mir the names of the new guards so she can add them as guests. Coll and I will let our wives know they aren't to come to Edinburgh."

Mirren was disappointed, but she understood that taking risks with the family wasn't an option. Still, that was the biggest event she'd ever planned, and she was disappointed that her mom, Jo, and her aunt Cat wouldn't be able to see her efforts. Plus, she was so damn proud of Finn's and Fiona's work and wanted to show it off.

"Charles, would you consider taking the girls home?" Coll asked.

Before her other dad could respond, there was a ruckus of little girl complaints. They must have been eavesdropping. Mirren approved. It was the best way to find out all the good information.

Blair must have signed something to her dad because Coll

said, "No, Kitten. You aren't in trouble for going into Mir's room, though you should have knocked first."

"It's because we saw Finny's bits, Blair," Mags groused.

Fiona snorted and slapped her hand over her mouth. Behind her, Finn said, "Please, God, not again."

Charles spoke over whatever else Mags was about to say. In one of the sternest tones Mirren had heard him use to date, he said, "Mags. You will stop speaking about Mr. Campbell's—"

Gray cut in. "Tadger."

"Tadger" was slang for "penis"—very naughty slang. That conversation was past going off the rails. Fiona was bent over, wheezing with laughter, and Mirren had to take the phone from Lyle's shaking hand; he had tucked his face in the crook of his elbow, which was poorly muffling his guffaws.

Her dad erupted with a "Jesus Christ, and just where have you heard such a word, young lady?"

Mirren could picture Gray with her arms crossed over her chest, not concerned by their dad's tone. "You called Uncle Colly one, and I asked Mommy what it meant."

They could hear Coll and her other dad cough-laughing in the background when her dad said, "Did Mommy tell you not to repeat it?" After a pause, he added, "It isn't a nice word."

"Can I say 'bits and bobs,' then?" Gray asked sweetly.

Sighing heavily, her dad answered, "I would prefer we not discuss private parts." And then, "We'll ask Mommy about that."

"She calls it a penis. I think that's American," Mags added.

Her dad, Charles, had the final say. "Enough of that now. You three lassies run to your room and pack, and if you're quick about it, we'll stop by a McDonald's for french fries, and if you're really, really fast, maybe an ice cream."

Squeals of joy and the trampling of little feet running up the stairs followed the announcement. Hopefully, family conversations involving Finn's "bits and bobs" would finally shrivel and die a quick death.

"Before I hang up," Mirren started, mentally patting herself on the back for her even tone, "I would like to say that I hope you three can manage to stop talking about your privates in front of the little ones."

"Maybe you shouldn't be sharing your shower," her dad snapped back.

Mirren could tell he was gritting his teeth. "I'll stop when you stop," she countered.

Charles interrupted. "I'm sorry we'll miss your show and seeing Finn's and Fiona's exhibits, Mir. Promise to call Mom and me and tell us everything."

"I'm so disappointed everyone can't come, but I understand. I promise to take pictures and videos and tell you everything." Once Mirren hung up and handed the phone back to Lyle, she knew by the sly glances on his and Fiona's faces that she and Finn were about to get the teasing of their lives.

Fiona wiped her leaking eyes and was opening her mouth when Finn said, "No. No. I'm going to my shop."

As Finn stomped off, his sister called after him. "Oh, good, Finny. I bet there are a few 'bits and bobs' left to pack."

Mirren heard a faint "Dead to me" as Finn rounded the corner of the house.

She was pleased to see Lyle wrap his arm around Fiona's waist and how comfortable she was with the attention. "It sounds like you and my brother had an eventful morning," she teased.

By the time Mirren had described the embarrassing morning, starting with the shower scene and ending with the discussion in her kitchen, the four of them were handing the last of

Finn's exhibit pieces to the movers. All of the larger boxes held his metal sculptures that would double as displays for his jewelry. He wouldn't let her peek at the newest piece that he had worked on after leaving her bed the night before. *Patience,* she reminded herself.

"I can't wait to spend time with your sisters, Mirren, and your wee cousin, Blair," Fiona said, still snorting over Mirren's recounting.

"You say that, Fi, because you've only *heard* about the morning... You didn't *live* it," Finn said, frowning at his sister.

"And thank Christ for that," Lyle said, shaking his head, like he was shaking the very thought from his memory.

As the movers closed the truck, Fiona looked at Mirren, a serious look on her face. "Do you think Lance and his sister...do you think they know about...my past? Will they try to hurt me with it?"

Before Mirren could assure her, Lyle turned Fiona to face him. "I will never leave your side. Your brother will never leave your side. MacGregor and Barr will do their best to find the answers, but until they do, I want you to enjoy today. Enjoy your show. If your past were to come out, it would only prove that you're a survivor and fucking amazing. Give your worries to me."

A sigh gusted from Fiona, and she practically melted against Lyle's chest. "It isn't easy, but I'll give them to you."

"Probably because she likes Lyle's bits and bobs. Gross," Finn grumbled in Mirren's ear, making sure his sister heard.

The moment of sadness was thankfully washed away as Fiona whirled around and smacked Finn's shoulder. "You're such an ass."

"Mirren likes my ass," Finn rebutted like only a sibling could do.

"And Lyle likes mine. Sod off," Fiona huffed, but the twinkle in her eye tickled the group and they all laughed.

Mirren leaned into Finn's side and gave Fiona's hand a quick squeeze. "Let's go set up. Your exhibition awaits, and if I have anything to say about it...fame and fortune."

33

Hannah was furious about how well attended the Smith Gallery exhibition was but valiantly hiding her irritation behind a wide smile and a modest, high-necked knee-length gown. She had been wearing a zingier dress, still modest for appearances' sake, but it had been red and shimmery.

The voices had thought it was too flashy and made her take a sharp knife to her stomach, tearing the fabric and cutting the skin beneath. They thought it was funny that she'd had to change. They also loved seeing blood run down her stomach.

They could be such pricks. What was that saying from To Kill a Mockingbird? Something about a person being able to choose their friends but not their family. Truer words. The voices were unwanted, hateful, and spiteful... Still...they were hers.

She attempted to ignore the clear success of the evening for the Campbell twins, knowing damn well that her gallery didn't expect to see near the same numbers for her collection. She conversed with several important people about politics and art, of course. Her mother was distantly related to the British royal family but not too distant to impress. Her mother was her father's second wife.

Her dear old dad had clearly married up. He'd been a carpenter for her mother's wealthy family, which was why he'd ended up throwing Hannah's half-brother's mom to the curb. Lance's mother had had to start selling real estate, and not even nice properties, to make ends meet. Her dear old dead dad had been a right grasping, money-hungry prick. She would give him some credit though. He had created Lance.

Her older brother had been a wonderful source of information when it had come to learning the names of some of her competitors. Lance had been trying his hand at sleuthing out stories, convinced he would be the next greatest investigative reporter. Perhaps he could be. After all, he'd done a hell of a job ferreting out salacious tidbits about the artists competing against his sister.

He'd meant it as a bit of fun to help his little sister out after she'd begged him so prettily, though in his mind, it had turned into a chance to impress his employer with his skill and tenacity. Once he had decided that that might be his big break, he had stopped telling Hannah anything.

He hadn't expected her to steal into his house and find out the really good stuff.

He would pay for putting himself first.

She had expected to see Lance tonight. He was one of the main journalists covering the art world for the Daily Mail. Not that she gave a shit. Hannah only pretended to care about him because he'd written really good pieces about her work over the past few years—he was a useful douchebag.

Spying one of her mother's elderly cousins, Robert Hilton, across the room, she changed her mind about getting another drink and made her way over to where he was admiring one of the artist's paintings.

Fiona Campbell was a genius. Hannah would give her that,

but no amount of talent would save her from her little daddy secret.

She smiled demurely at Robert, catching his attention. The man was a class A asshole with a mean streak a mile wide. There had been rumors for years that the fat narcissist was abusive to his wife.

It was off topic to that night's goals, but why didn't his wife leave him? It wasn't like she couldn't outrun the man with minimal effort. Pathetic. She deserved what she got.

There was one really wonderful thing about Robert that could always be counted on, and that was his absolute love for gossip. One minute of his time, and the whole room would be panting with the Campbell scandal.

"Robert. It's so good to see you."

34

———

orvus. Mirren was still ridiculously pleased with the name of Finn's exhibit, which the stubborn asshole had refused to divulge before the show, even for press releases. "Corvus" in Latin represented a genus of birds, namely crows, rooks, and ravens.

Ravens. She let her fingers glide over the ravens at her wrists, neck, ears, and fingers. Mirren wore a long black slip dress that poured over her curves like a still midnight river. The cowl neck created a perfect frame. Her hair was in a simple, sleek bun at her nape.

She'd made herself into a canvas, an elegant backdrop to showcase Finn's stunning raven collection. She couldn't wait for people to ask her about the set. *Oh, yes, I own the entire collection, and Mr. Campbell is mine too.*

Finn watched her walk down the stairs that evening. It was his first glimpse of her since he'd gotten ready at his house. His first look if their meeting secretly in his old workshop behind her house an hour and a half ago didn't count.

She'd been in her bedroom, laying out the evening's outfit,

when her phone had chimed with a notification. A text from Finn.

I miss you.

Rolling her eyes but secretly thrilled, she had replied,

You've only been gone an hour.

You're addictive.

She'd sat on the bed and pulled her legs beneath her, considering what to reply.

What are you most addicted to?

Wavy dots had waved and waved and waved as he'd answered her. Finally, his reply had appeared.

Your eyes are addictive. Your attitude, your wit, your intelligence.

Wavy dots.

Making you food. Watching you making tea. How you love your family…and mine. Your smile… I want to see it every day. All day.

Her heart had been pounding. Finn had really been pulling out all the best boyfriend moves. She had been about to respond with something equally romantic when more wavy dots had appeared.

He hadn't been done with his list.

Your hand in mine. Your body is a work of art.

Another message had followed.

> My body leaning over yours. The way you look
> with your head thrown back as you ride me.
> The taste of your mouth. The taste between
> your legs. Your face when I make you come.

He'd gone from romance to spice. She'd approved. Mirren had crossed her legs when she'd read the last of his list, her sex instantly throbbing with need. She'd known then that Finn would be lucky if she didn't drag him to her office for a quickie during the event.

> Meet me in my workshop behind your house.
> I'm already here.

Had the lunatic thought she would be able to casually sneak out of the house for a hookup under the noses of her dad and uncle?

> Please. I'm so hard, I can't think straight. I
> went home, but all I could think of was sinking
> into your body.

> Finn! My dad!

> I'll make it good for you, I swear.

She'd looked at the time. She had been about to reply, considering all the ways it could go embarrassingly wrong, when a final text had come through.

> And fast.

> You're impossible. Be there in two.

She'd been grinning as she'd jogged down the stairs and gone straight to the laundry room, where she had hoped to slip out without a confrontation.

She'd been about to go out the door when a dreaded voice had sounded behind her. "Going somewhere, Mir Mir?"

Damn it! Her uncle Coll had seen her. Keeping her hand on the doorknob, she had turned. "Finn thinks he might have left something in the shop out back. I'm just going to take a look around and let him know if I find it before I get around to tonight." That had sounded legit. Maybe.

"He must not trust you to find the... What was it he misplaced?"

Think. Think. Think. "A suit pin. He made it for himself." *Brilliant!*

"Did Campbell tell you he's already in the shop *searching* for the missing pin?"

She hadn't risen to her uncle's snarky baiting. "Of course."

"Should your dad and I come to help? It sounds like finding it might be a needle in a haystack situation."

Enough had been enough. "Not necessary." She'd opened the laundry room door and stepped out. Over her shoulder, she'd said, "See you soon—but not too soon, if you know what I mean." Coll's growled "Mirren Mòr" had had her grinning as she'd rushed to Finn's old shop.

He must have seen her coming because the door had opened before her feet had hit the small cobblestone apron that wrapped around the entrance. Finn's handsome face had been intent. His eyes had watched her every step as she'd moved close to his body, his long arm moving past her to shut and lock the door at her back.

He'd bent and kissed the crease of her neck. The light sucks and licks had sent shivers up her spine. She'd grasped the sides of his head and dragged his mouth to hers, moaning as he'd taken what she had offered.

The kiss had been insistent and hot. His hands had caressed her hips and thighs, following the curve of her waist around her back and to her breasts.

Her hardened nipples had scraped repeatedly against the silk of her bralette. They had both been frantic, sharing moans and praises. She'd skimmed her hands over his chest, pulling the material up until he'd broken the kiss to rip the tee over his head.

Her fingers had traced his abs, continuing until she could follow the ridge of his sex. The thick outline had looked uncomfortable behind the fly of his jeans. He'd let her play for another minute, pumping against her hand while his tongue used the same rhythm in her mouth.

He'd been slowly backing her toward the one soft piece of furniture in the shop, an old floral-printed couch. He'd sat first and tugged her body against his chest, where she'd brought her knees up to straddle his lap.

His voice hoarse with desire, he had confessed, "I need hours to do what I want with you."

Kissing the side of his neck, she had tunneled her fingers through his thick dark-red beard. She'd given him a light kiss. "We have ten minutes, or we'll be late to your own exhibition."

"Fuck the exhibition. I need hours," he'd repeated against her lips, holding her hips as she undulated against his hardness.

"Nine minutes now," she had said as she'd pulled her shirt off, taking the bralette with it. He'd instantly sucked one of her nipples into his mouth. "Christ, Finn, just like that." He had alternated between her breasts, pinching and pulling and sucking.

Breaking the kiss, she'd demanded, "Let me up. We only have minutes, man, minutes! Clothes off as quick as you can!"

Had anyone seen the frenzy with which they'd shucked off the rest of their clothes, they would have thought she and Finn had been mad. When he'd sat down again, he'd still had one sock on; the other had been barely hanging on to his toes.

The moment her own joggers and panties had come off, she'd been back in his lap, a sigh and a "Mmm" falling from her mouth as their centers aligned.

"Tonight, when you're walking around the gallery, smiling and laughing and being the perfect host, I'm going to picture you just like this—naked and spread across my lap."

His fingers had glided lightly down her throat and between her breasts. She had shifted on his lap enough for him to guide himself inside her. She'd gasped as he'd slowly worked his length home, stealing her moan in a deep kiss.

Mirren had rolled her hips slowly, groaning each time his length hit all the sensitive places deep inside. She'd slapped her hands on his shoulders and ridden him like they'd had all the time in the world.

"Feels so good, baby. Christ, I could stay in you forever."

As he'd taken control of the pace, she hadn't been able to stop the small cries she had made when he'd hit that spot deep inside her harder and faster than she'd managed. She had felt her orgasm starting to cramp her belly and leaned back, resting her palms on his knees, letting her hair drape down her back and touch his thighs. Her movements had started to become jerky, and a constant chant of "Finn, Finn, Finn, Finn" had been her only language.

"If I had the ability, I would sketch you as you are at this moment," he had growled, his voice rough with passion and exertion.

She'd emitted a long, sharp cry as her body had shaken with tremors, tremendous pulses lighting up her sex—squeezing Finn until his own shout followed.

He'd stroked her damp back as she'd laid her forehead on his shoulder. Eventually, their breathing had evened, and their skin had cooled.

Finn had spoken quietly in her ear, not wanting to disturb the peace any more than she did. "I would sculpt you with your head thrown back and your mouth open as you screamed my name, coming undone around me."

Mirren had smiled at his description of her. Even during such a mind-blowing intimate moment, Finn had seen the world–and her, apparently—through the lens of an artist.

Kissing his shoulder, she had sat up, her inner muscles tightening once more at the shift, causing Finn to suck air through his teeth. "Do that again, lass, and you won't be leaving this room anytime soon."

Chuckling, she had said, "If it were any night but this night, I wouldn't let you leave this room for a week. But alas…" She'd slid from his lap, separating their bodies with a hiss as her sensitized flesh felt the friction of their bodies unraveling.

Taking a quick step back to avoid Finn's grasping hands, she had laughed. "I have to go or there won't be a single person at the event who doesn't know exactly what we've been doing."

"Better the guests than MacGregor or Barr, I'd say."

"Unfortunately, their observation skills are top notch. Staying virginal wasn't a priority for me but a matter of having no opportunity. I had to have been the most tracked child in Bunchrew, possibly Scotland. Once, I was convinced Dad had to have a mic on me and tore apart my backpack looking for one." She'd laughed again.

Mirren had noticed him side-eyeing her Bob Ross socks. "You better not even think of bad-mouthing one of the most iconic artists in the world, Finn."

He'd put his hands up in surrender. "Fi and I used to watch Bob Ross reruns at the public library. No hate, I swear. Only"—

he had paused with an exaggerated sigh and headshake—"it was a little disconcerting to have the man grinning at me the whole time you rode me. A bit X-rated for the man's tastes, surely."

Mirren had snorted. "Don't be an ass. Bob would say we were happy people doing happy things."

She'd dressed quickly, trying to ignore Finn's muscles flexing as he did the same. She had been rushing toward the exit when she'd remembered something. "If you have a man's brooch not in the collection tonight, wear it. Please." And then she had been gone, running into the back laundry.

Two hours later, Mirren was descending the stairs at her house, hopefully straddling the line between orgasmic glow and sophistication.

If his appreciative look was any indication, Finn approved. If she needed further validation, the moment she was by his side, he lightly rested his hands on her sides and bent to whisper, "You outshine every diamond in my collection."

She kissed his cheek before he pulled away, making a show of looking him up and down. "My goodness, Mr. Campbell, you're a handsome sight." He was wearing a sharp black suit paired with a soft T-shirt that was a gorgeous mix of copper and bronze.

The tee must have been a nod to his collection's palette. The metal sculptures ranged between smooth and hammered bronze, which he cleverly used to showcase his jewelry.

The jewelry collection took her breath away, and she had no doubt the guests that evening would be wowed as well. Some pieces were finely layered copper of the finest, most delicate strands. One particular brooch could have been worn by both men and women. He'd created a fine braided frame around a large irregularly shaped dark-brown cassiterite stone.

His collection was large and varied but cohesive for all that. It had nods to heraldry, but the meticulously carved animals, especially the unicorns, softened many of the pieces, creating a sense of fantasy.

Mirren was blown away. She could have walked between the displays for hours and still not discovered all their secrets. The final piece Finn had created the night they'd first made love had yet to be placed on his separate display podium. He had said it was a surprise and wouldn't reveal it until right before the party. *Tease.*

She was about to insist he kiss her properly, sliding her hands around his waist and rising on her tiptoes, when the obnoxious sound of tandem throat-clearing graced her hearing. Sighing, she looked around Finn and found her uncle and dad glaring at them both.

Determined not to let the fun-hating Debbi Downers' crap dull her shine, she boosted herself as high as her low-heeled sandals allowed and gave Finn a smacking kiss regardless of their audience.

"Did you call your mom and...dad?" Her dad still struggled, after all those years, to refer to Charles as "dad." She didn't blame him. He'd been her only father for sixteen years, and he hadn't been looking for help or a replacement when Charles had come along.

She'd had to reassure him often in the first two years since Charles's arrival that their relationship was unchanged. Her mother had happened to love a man whose sperm had created Mirren, and even though Mirren had been open to forming a loving relationship with Charles Morrow, Thomas MacGregor was *Dad.*

She called Charles "Dad" as well because Mirren had come to love and respect him greatly. She also knew that had he known his ex-girlfriend was pregnant, he would never have stayed away.

"Yes, I did, *Dad.* I showed them my dress and—"

"Which is way too revealing for someone her age," Coll groused under his breath.

Ignoring him as usual, she continued. "Promised to call later. I called Jo too. Grandma Mary said I looked like a princess." She grinned, making Finn chuckle and the other two grunt, but she saw her dad's lips twitch.

He reluctantly admitted, "You look lovely, Mir. A tad grown up for my taste but lovely."

Showing no concern for their audience, Finn added, "You do look like a princess." Enveloping her hand in his, he tugged her to his side and ran a finger over the raven at her neck. He really liked her wearing his art.

Finn's serious expression as he studied her made Mirren's stomach flutter. She really, really, really would love to skip the gallery and drag Finn to her bedroom, strip him naked, and make him show her all the ways a man could make a woman orgasm. She also really, really, really hoped none of her thoughts showed on her face.

Hoping to redirect everyone's attention from her flushed cheeks, Mirren asked, "Nothing on Lance Merte?"

"No, but we're having to be very careful not to step on any toes. The detectives on the case are taking great care to piece together ties between the man found in the motel room and the other incidents involving the other artists," her dad explained.

"They are doing a meticulous job from what Tommy and I have seen," Coll added. "Outside interference from MacGregor Security would not be welcome. We did discover that Merte bought train tickets from the Edinburgh Waverly train station online the morning the body was discovered."

"What was the destination?" Finn asked.

"London. No return ticket, but that doesn't mean anything. He could just as easily buy a return ticket at the station. They aren't looking too hard for him yet since they have no evidence of his or his sister's involvement."

Mirren shuddered as she grabbed her black clutch for the evening. "I'm still holding out hope that neither of them is involved. Hell, I hope all the strange occurrences in Scotland's art community are truly coincidental." She watched her dad and uncle exchange a look. They had no such hope.

"There's nothing to be done tonight except to enjoy all your hard work, Mir," Finn announced as he wrapped an arm around her shoulders and pulled her gently against his side.

She shook her head and laughed. "I agree to enjoying the night, but you and Fiona did all the work. Between your sister's paintings and your exquisite jewelry and stunning metal sculptures, Smith Gallery's showroom has never looked so posh.

"I admit that I can't wait to get there before the doors officially open so I can do one more walkthrough. And you have one last piece to display, you jerk."

She elbowed his side, attempting to look mad. His smirk said he found her amusing. She caught her dad giving Finn a strange look. It wasn't irritation, but there was something odd about it. Finn went still at her side, and his smile flattened. *What the hell?*

Looking between them once more, Mirren announced they really had to leave. Her dad and her uncle Coll led the way to their SUV. They needed the room since they were picking up Fiona, Lyle, and the two new guards, Sloan and May. As her dad maneuvered through traffic, the mood in the vehicle was electric with excitement.

Fiona was wearing a stunning slate wrap dress, which paired perfectly with Lyle's dark navy slacks and sweater. She got teary-eyed when they picked her up and she saw Mirren wearing her brother's ravens. Dabbing at her eyes, Fiona whispered through her tears, "It means the world to me, Finn, that the *Unkindness* you sacrificed to help me ended up in the hands of the woman you love."

Both she and Finn froze for a moment at having the L word bandied about so casually. When her dad's eyes flicked to Mirren's in the rearview mirror, she averted her gaze immediately.

"Fortuitous" was Finn's only verbal response.

35

Finn was a nervous, disgusting, sweaty mess—and it had nothing to do with the crowd circling his exhibit. It didn't even have to do with the grand entrance of the museum's judges. He was a pragmatic man. They would like his work or they wouldn't.

He couldn't help but glance at his last entry, the piece he'd finished after he and Mirren had made a verbal commitment to one another as well as a physical one—if having sex for hours counted, which it very well did.

Finn was a man of many interests. Jewelry making and sculpting, of course, plus cooking and reading. He had only one obsession: Mirren MacGregor. She *was* his obsession, addiction, and muse. Each handcrafted piece in his collection held a bit of that MacGregor imp's essence.

Turning back to the crowd, he watched her work the room as she smiled and laughed, encouraging the art enthusiasts to enjoy the night. He could have watched her for hours, even after MacGregor had caught Finn eye-stalking his daughter more than once. One would have thought the man would lighten up, considering their earlier talk.

He thanked another person for their enthusiasm over his collection and immediately went back to scanning the gallery. His twin was speaking to one of the judges, her face a mixture of seriousness and passion. Finn knew she would win the oil division. Her collection was spectacular.

Artists didn't have to name their works or exhibits, but he and Fi had decided to name theirs. Her exhibit was called *Surviving*. She'd told him it wasn't about her surviving but rather how she views her subjects as she paints. "Every day that a person gets up and makes a decision to live, to walk, to laugh, to fall in love...make mistakes, it's surviving."

Finn's was called *Corvus* simply because his ravens had led him to that moment. The final piece had its own name: $4M+C$. He'd carved it in the palm of the last metal sculpture he'd presented. He'd heard several people wondering whether it had to do with time, like Roman numerals.

Only he and Thomas MacGregor knew the meaning. Soon, *she* would know.

Mirren Mòr MacGregor-Morrow + Campbell.

Finn had sculpted the partial arm of a woman out of bronze months ago. The soft skin and delicate underside of the wrist were feminine and alluring. The sculpture lay with the palm facing up and the fingers curled slightly in a natural resting pose. He'd carved twin ravens facing each other on the wrist. Originally, he hadn't thought the sculpture fit in with his collection, so he had abandoned it.

That was before Mirren had agreed to be his. Before he'd made her his.

Before he'd understood the hand represented her—that the simple oval cut brown diamond that he'd set in the narrowest of gold bands with delicate prongs had always been meant for Mirren, and he couldn't imagine a more dramatic way for her to first see it—though she had no idea it was meant for her.

The sculpture with the ring was his collection's pièce de résistance. It represented the whole of *Corvus*. When Mirren had asked him about the meaning behind it, he'd only shrugged, which had earned him an elbow to the side.

By the end of the evening, she would know exactly what it stood for and exactly who the ring's intended owner was—and, God, he hoped he hadn't miscalculated her feelings.

Catching MacGregor's glare from across the room once more, Finn steeled his expression and his spine. He'd told Mirren's father what his plans for the evening were a few hours before he'd met her in his old workshop—actually, he had told MacGregor and her uncle Coll, who'd invited himself. Barr had leaned against the side of the house, watching them, his arms crossed over his broad chest and a scowl slashing his mouth.

His knees had threatened to knock. A testament to how intimidating the two men could be, but Finn hadn't let their posturing put him off. He hadn't backed down from anything after he and his sister had run from Edinburgh all those years before.

He hadn't told Mirren that he'd spoken to her father because he didn't want to ruin the surprise. Or that's what he'd told himself. The real, real reason was because he'd let an annoying string of doubts creep in. Was he going too fast? She was several years younger. Should he wait? Would she embrace that level of commitment or let him down gently?

Once he'd been sure Mirren had retreated to her office that afternoon to make last-minute calls and go over her checklists for the event another hundred times, he had texted MacGregor, asking him to step outside and meet him by his truck. Thirty seconds later, both he and Barr had exited the front door. Barr had stayed back while MacGregor had slowly walked toward the truck to meet him.

He'd lifted a brow in question at Finn, not willing to break the tense silence. That had been fine by him.

Taking a fortifying breath, Finn hadn't started slow and easy. "I love Mirren." He'd watched in fascination as a ruddy hue had spread rapidly over the big man's fair skin. Finn had decided not to immediately follow up his first verbal volley. MacGregor had needed a moment to digest the announcement.

After huffing a few breaths in and out and clenching and unclenching his fists, Mirren's dad had asked, "Do you, now?"

"Yes."

"Does she know how you feel?"

"Not completely," Finn had admitted.

"And how does Mir feel about you?"

Well, that's the question, isn't it? "I believe... I think..." Finn had shaken his head at the fumbling nonsense coming from his mouth. He'd known that stuttering bullshit wouldn't convince MacGregor that he was the man for his daughter. Truth then.

"I hope she feels the same." It was safe to say that his hope rivaled the sun in its intensity.

Finn had stood straighter, not willing to appear weak. *Come to the point, jackass,* he'd chided himself. "I have a ring. I mean, I made a ring. For her. Mirren, that is." *Have mercy and smite me down, God.*

"And?" MacGregor had growled.

"I want to ask her to marry me tonight. After the show."

"And?" the bastard had parroted again.

"I want your approval." And because he was a man with equal amounts of bravado, nerve, and pride himself, he'd added, "I'll still ask her. With or without it."

The saying "You could cut the tension with a knife" hadn't faced down a protective father. A claymore sword couldn't have cut through the black currents of conflict circling the two men.

Minutes or hours had passed. Finn had stood resolute in the

face of an ancient warrior protecting one of his most valued possessions.

"I will make you disappear if you hurt her," MacGregor had finally relented.

Finn had known that his hopefully soon-to-be father-in-law was being serious, but he'd taken the man's threat because, with it, MacGregor had also given his permission.

"If I ever hurt Mirren, I would deserve nothing less."

Finn had noticed Coll had moved closer. MacGregor had suddenly stuck his hand out to shake. In less than a blink, Finn had clasped the offered firm grasp and had to swallow his emotion at the momentous moment.

"I'm a man who's always plowed his own course, Campbell, whether with a hoe or explosives. Nothing would have kept me from my sweet Josephine, and if you feel a fraction of what I do for Jo for my daughter, then you're one lucky sonofabitch if she says yes."

Approval. It was at once a single word and an opus.

He'd meant what he'd said. He would have made Mirren his own with or without that man's consent, but Christ, it had felt good to receive it. He'd clasped the man's strong grip again and dipped his head in appreciation.

After receiving back slaps from both men, Finn had watched them turn and walk back toward the house. He'd heard Barr say to his best friend, "Christ, Brother, you've gone soft." Clearly, not true.

MacGregor had only huffed a laugh. "You must be aware, Brother, that your wee Blair is exactly like her momma. I don't recall my sister doing anything but exactly what she wanted."

Barr's "Shit" was the last word Finn had heard before the door had closed behind them. That's when he'd made his way to the back of the house and tried to convince Mirren to meet him.

Right then, there he was, a jittery mess, wishing to hell the evening was over so he could remove that beautiful brown diamond ring from the sculpture's ring finger and slip it onto Mirren's.

Noting that Mirren had made her way to his sister and Lyle, who was standing protectively at her side, Finn couldn't stop his feet from taking him across the room. He wasn't paying that close of attention to the guests or servers carrying platters of champagne flutes at first, but there was something...a shift in the conversation flow. There was more than one group with heads close together, whispering. He even received a few startled glances when they noticed him passing.

He felt the hair on the back of his neck stiffen. Something was off. He searched until he found MacGregor's bodyguards, Sloan and May. They had kept to the periphery of the room most of the night, but they were meandering through the crowd, slowly but deliberately moving toward MacGregor and Barr.

Abandoning his move toward Mirren, he followed the bodyguards. The women were speaking quietly when he arrived, and the looks of fury that crossed the men's faces had Finn's stomach dropping.

Before he could ask, MacGregor leaned forward and spoke quietly to Finn. "Someone has been working the room, spreading hateful gossip about what happened to Fiona." MacGregor quickly grabbed Finn's arm, stopping him from gathering his sister and getting her the hell out of there.

"Don't stop me," Finn warned.

"Wait one minute, for Christ's sake." He looked at his friend. "Coll. Go to Lyle now. Sloan. May. Lead Fiona and Lyle out using the back exit. Finn, trust Lyle to protect your sister. Get to Mirren and have her round up the judges. Things are about to get ugly, and she'll know best how to handle the crowd."

Finn took a deep breath, knowing MacGregor was right. "Where will you be?"

"I'm going to find that bitch, Hannah Todd. She has to be responsible."

As the two men separated, it became immediately apparent that they were too late.

Far too fucking late.

Finn noticed several things at once. Fi's face was still, and she looked utterly crushed. Lyle, Sloan, and May had their hands on her, urging her to move. Mirren and her father were rushing toward the middle of the gallery, and finally, Hannah Todd was clapping her hands and sweetly asking for everyone's attention.

MacGregor reached Hannah first and was in the process of using his big body to move her back without laying a hand on her when… "No, Thomas. Let Ms. Todd have her moment. It seems she's been diligently preparing for it this evening."

Fiona shook off Lyle's and the bodyguards' hands, taking several steps forward, a martyr prepared to stand alone. *Screw that.* While everyone else in attendance appeared frozen, Finn quickly joined his sister, shoulder to shoulder. Murmurs, clinking crystal, and even breaths were suspended.

Hannah Todd was momentarily taken aback, but it didn't take long for her false persona of a charming society woman and local artist to help her transform her lips, thinned with displeasure, and her narrowed eyes into a macabre excuse for humbleness. She even went so far as to shrug apologetically to the three confused judges standing nearby.

"Forgive the interruption, but it's come to the guests' attention that Fiona Campbell has quite the colorful past—too colorful for such an esteemed institution as the Scottish National Gallery of Modern Art." Hannah pretended to blanch for the judges' benefit. "Perhaps, gentlemen, you might want to retire for the evening. I'm sure everyone here can agree that it's time to call it an evening, and Ms. Campbell would probably like a chance to clear"—she paused and coughed delicately against her fingers, as if she were embarrassed—"certain... things up."

Finn was about to tell Hannah Todd to go fuck herself when one of the judges, the youngest one, Jenson Paul, raised a hand and solemnly said, "A moment, please," instantly gaining the room's attention.

"I won't speak for Harold and Basil," Jenson continued, nodding to the two other judges, "but I'm not going anywhere until someone explains this nonsense." He looked sternly at Hannah before adding, "And as this isn't your evening, Ms. Todd, I think it poor taste of you to interrupt a fellow artist's event."

As reprimands went, Jenson's deserved an award. The flare of red slashing Hannah's cheeks was satisfying.

Before Finn could move his sister somewhere less conspicuous and Mirren could do her magic and put the guests back in the mood to study art instead of gossip, Hannah actually stomped her foot and clapped her hands for attention.

"I can assure you, *Mr. Paul*," she snarled, losing her cool demeanor completely, "I would despise myself if you were not made immediately aware of what type of woman you are considering for the competition. Campbell is a fine artist—there's no denying her skill—but surely, you wouldn't choose a woman who flagrantly had a sexual relationship with her own father. Is that the type of artist you would encourage families to visit your museum to see?!"

Gasps, cries of distress, and sounds of shattering glass echoed about the room. Finn twisted toward Lyle, who was already on the move. "Take Fi, please. Just go." Looking at his sister, Finn knew he had seen more life in Strazza's famous *The*

Veiled Virgin bust, but where the *Virgin* looked peaceful, Fiona was quiet and still. Lifeless.

Placing his hand against her cold white cheek, he pleaded, "Please, Fi. Leave now."

Her eyes flicked briefly to her brother's, and finally, finally, Finn saw her chest move with breath. "No."

He felt deep in his chest that his twin would not be moved. Fine, then, he would work to clear everyone else from the room. The first to be thrown out on their ass would be Hannah Todd, but his fearless Mirren was already on it.

Pointing a finger at the woman who had caused the entire mess, who was, at that moment, stretching her lips unnaturally wide in a creepy smile, Mirren said, "You are no longer welcome. Get out." Then she grabbed her dad's hand. "Would you make sure she finds her way outside, Dad?"

As Finn approached Mirren, the owners of Smith Gallery did too. Kain looked only at Hannah but raised his voice so the room could hear. "You are banned from setting foot in any Smith family-owned galleries, Ms. Todd, and I think you'll be surprised at just how many there are, how respected our name is, and how easy it will be to encourage others to do the same."

Then Kain's sister, Lillias, spoke, her even voice devoid of inflection. "Your behavior tonight was disgusting and intolerable. Leave." Then she slowly turned, making eye contact with several chagrined-looking guests. "If anyone else shares this woman's views, please find your way out as well."

Finn grasped Mirren's hand and squeezed, mouthing, "Thank you." She nodded with a wobbly smile, her eyes wet with unshed tears.

MacGregor crowded Hannah, who was laughing as though the whole evening had been great fun. Mirren looked startled. "She's not...right."

"Definitely not," Finn agreed.

MacGregor growled, "Get going, Ms. Todd, or we'll be forced to ring the police and have you removed for trespassing."

"That won't be necessary," another voice sounded from the front door.

The crowd turned to find that three officers and Lance Merte, of all people, had entered. Finn quickly glanced in his sister's direction. Lyle, Coll, and the two new guards were surrounding her still. Relieved, he turned back to the police and Lance, only to see Hannah clapping her hands and squealing in delight before jogging toward them.

"Lance! I'm so glad you were able to make it!" She completely ignored the officers at her brother's back.

Lance shuddered, looking disgusted at her behavior, and took a step back before her hands could touch him. A short, stocky officer blocked Hannah's path. "Hannah Todd, you are under arrest..."

Ten minutes of shock and awe later, a screaming and hand-cuffed Hannah was out the door and being loaded into a police cruiser at the curb, all while reporters yelled questions and camera flashes blinked like raining stars.

Lance stayed behind to explain—after several minutes of sobbed apologies—that he had begun to suspect that Hannah was behind several of the artist's misfortunes. He admitted to bragging to his sister that he'd uncovered most of the artists in the competition and even some useful gossip to spice up his next piece for the newspaper he worked for.

"I soon realized my mistake in revealing anything to her. Hannah is my father's daughter with his second wife. She was decent as a kid, but she was involved in a horrible car accident as a young teen, and Dad told me that he believed the head trauma that she incurred...I don't know, changed her.

"She became secretive. Her moods were erratic. One minute, she was kind and laughing and asking me to lunch.

Then months or years later, if I passed her on the street, she would pretend not to know me.

"I'm embarrassed to admit that I bragged about my grand plans to become an investigative reporter instead of a simple social writer—that I was amazing. She dared me to prove it by finding out who her competition for the museum exhibit would be. She goaded me by saying I wasn't good enough to find out shit."

"You proved her wrong," Mirren stated. Her usual smile was missing, and her shoulders were drooping after the evening's fiasco.

"I did, and if I could take it back, burn everything before she got her eyes on it, I would. It didn't take me long to realize that I could never use my writing to hurt people. I love art, and I love writing about it. I'm good at it, and I pray my own stupidity and my relationship with Hannah haven't ruined that for me."

He explained that after he'd started suspecting Hannah, he'd tried to reach Hannah's mother for weeks, but she had never answered or called him back. Hannah had told him she was still visiting friends in London. "She tried to hide it, but she was angry at me when I brought it up a second time. She told me to mind my own family and that her mother didn't even like me or my mother. I knew that wasn't true. We weren't close, but Sue was always kind to me.

"I went to London and discovered she wasn't there. Her friend told me that she had been out of the country for half a year and had only gotten back home a few days earlier. She felt terrible that she'd only tried to reach Sue a few times. When her friend hadn't answered, she'd just assumed their timing was off."

Believing Hannah might have done something to her mother, Lance had gone to the police and told them everything. How he'd researched the artists for an article. How he believed his sister had sneaked into his apartment and found his research, especially the information he hadn't told her about.

"Like what happened to my sister?" Finn growled.

Lance blanched when he met Finn's furious face. "I don't expect you to believe me, but even had I done an exposé on the contestants, I would never have included your sister's history. What I discovered... When I realized what... The neighbor's account... It's when I knew I could never write such painful things for public fodder." He looked at Fiona. "I don't expect forgiveness, but I truly am sorry."

Probably the most shocking revelation of the night was when Lance revealed that after he'd insisted on performing a wellness check on Hannah's mother, he and the police had found the poor woman near death, chained to a painting desk in the attic of her and Hannah's home. The older woman had been malnourished, dehydrated, forced to use an overfilled bucket to relieve herself, and forced to paint. Hannah's paintings were really her mother's. It was so sinful and sickening. It pained all of them to think of the agony that poor woman had endured.

Fi didn't speak, but she did give the man a brief nod of acknowledgment for his apology, which was more than the ruddy bastard deserved.

Finn bent to kiss Mirren's cheek before he took hold of his sister's hands. "I'm sorry your big night was ruined, Fi." He felt the lump in his throat acutely when he saw the sad look on his twin's face.

Swallowing her own lump of emotion, Fiona retorted, "It was your big night too, you clod."

36

"'Pride goeth before destruction, and an haughty spirit before a fall,'" one voice announced, a definite smirking tone present.

"I find a certain pleasure in finding out a person's worth through their actions."

"Worthless people produce worthless outcomes."

"Think of the fun prison will be. I bet a lot of women will find Hannah fascinating."

"I bet the other inmates like to play rough like we do," a giggling voice chirped.

"They'll be disappointed, as we all have been for years. Her fellow inmates will find out soon enough that she isn't worth the air she breathes."

"We've spent years trying to make something from nothing."

"And she's still nothing."

"Pray for a mental institution. This pathetic excuse of a woman will give so many psychologists hours of jackoff material."

"Truth."

"Agreed."

"*Shut your stupid mouth, bitch, and start crying. Screeching like an imbecile will get us nowhere.*"

"*Silent and soft.*"

"*Broken and repentant.*"

Hannah listened to the disloyal voices in her head and stopped screaming, resting her cheek against the cold glass in the back of the police car.

She'd always listened. Always minded.

If she did get into an institution, maybe she could even paint again.

They might even let her go eventually. She had killed that man only to make the voices happy. They would definitely see that she hadn't wanted to harm anyone and let her go.

Maybe. Someday.

She only needed to cry. Softly. Softly. Softly.

37

Mirren stepped forward and thanked Lance again for going to the police before smoothly leading him to the gallery's entrance and wishing him the best. As she turned back to the room, she sighed at the guests' unease.

When Lance had been explaining everything, Mirren had beckoned to Mr. Tall and asked him to listen to what Mr. Merte had to say. Hopefully, he'd done as she'd asked and was even then letting his brother, the guests, and—most importantly—the judges know that the police believed Hannah was the one responsible for the crimes against her competitors.

The Smith siblings were doing their best to bring back the evening's earlier gaiety. It wasn't working. Mirren was about to walk to the judges and see whether there was any way to get the judging back on track when Fiona intercepted her.

"Mirren." She spoke quietly, lightly touching Mirren's arm.

Mirren was instantly fighting tears. She was crushed that Fiona's and Finn's work might not have gotten the chance to impress the judges and all the wealthy guests and art aficionados, but she was destroyed because Fiona's past had been revealed.

She ignored the tears pricking her eyes and tried to give Finn's sister a confident smile, but her wobbly lips surely ruined the effort. "I'm sorry, Fiona. Let me speak to the judges, but if you need to leave, please don't hesitate."

Fiona shook her head. "No. I don't know what Hannah told everyone, but I'm quite sure that she wouldn't have been satisfied with the truth. She wanted to hurt me, and she has, but she doesn't get to hurt my brother too. He might not have said so, but he wanted tonight as much as I did. I refuse to let that woman take it from us. From him."

Mirren didn't want Hannah to win either, but her hopes that the night could be salvaged were flagging. "So, would you like to speak with the judges with me?" Mirren glanced over her shoulder at Finn, who had joined them. He kissed the top of her head while placing his hands on her waist. She appreciated how stoic he had remained through all the disasters and leaned briefly against his chest, hoping to soak up some of his calm.

"I think our only chance of salvaging this mess is for me to speak."

"No way," Finn replied quickly.

"Yes," his sister countered. "And now, before I lose my nerve." Before Mirren or Finn could talk her out of whatever she had planned, Fiona joined the Smiths and exchanged a few brief words.

Kain cleared his throat and asked for the guests' attention. "No one can ever say the Smiths don't know how to create a memorable evening." The crowd chuckled. "One of the artists we're all here to celebrate would like to take this moment to speak to you." Lillias patted Fiona's hand before she and her brother backed away, giving Fi the floor.

Mirren felt Finn tense at her side. "Trust your sister, babe. If you believe in nothing else, believe that this night couldn't possibly get worse."

Fiona stood almost where Hannah had not very long before. Her impact on the crowd couldn't have been more different. A hush fell over the guests, and the judges all cocked their heads in interest. Fiona looked angelic, peaceful even, when her shaking hands were clasped at her waist. All eyes were riveted on her. She was as captivating as her art.

"Good evening. I am Fiona Campbell. I appreciate everyone who took the time to come tonight to see my brother's and my exhibits. Some of you I have already spoken to this evening, but many of you I haven't.

"Tonight has been...difficult, and I apologize for the level of... I'm sorry that any of you have had to endure any unpleasantness. Hannah Todd wanted to ruin my reputation and, ultimately, my chances to be chosen for a coveted spot in the Scottish National Gallery of Modern Art.

"I think we can all agree that though Ms. Todd's intentions were to harm, the woman is clearly not in her right mind."

Mirren looked at several guests who were nodding their heads in agreement. Fiona was doing well. Mirren was about to sigh in relief when Fiona's next words registered.

"Ms. Todd maliciously spread lies, hurting me and hurting my brother." Fiona briefly glanced at Finn with a look of resignation. "However, even though her version of my past was false, I do have one. A past, that is."

A few people tittered and attempted to smile, understanding that Fiona was trying to add a drop of levity.

"Our father"—she nodded briefly toward her twin, even though there was no mistaking their shared heritage—"was an alcoholic and a drug addict. He beat our mother regularly. She died when Finn and I were little.

"Dad was mean and hateful and unpredictable. My brother always took the brunt of his abuse—his fists. If Finn and I didn't work, we didn't eat. We planned on moving out the moment we turned eighteen."

Mirren felt tears running down her face, and many others in the room were dabbing at their eyes with cocktail napkins. She glanced at her father, surely one of the best men in the world, and wished that men like Thomas MacGregor were the norm and not the exception.

"What Ms. Todd discovered was that when I was sixteen—"

"Don't, Fi. You don't have to say," Finn pleaded.

"If I tell my story on my terms, Brother, then no one else can tell it for me. You have protected me my whole life. Let me do this." Finn squeezed his eyes shut, his mouth a firm line of aching despair, but eventually, he opened his eyes and nodded his acceptance.

"When I was sixteen, Dad caught me alone at a coffee shop near our apartment building and dragged me home. I had been waiting for Finn inside because it was raining, and a few of the waitresses were kind enough to let me sit inside without ordering.

"I don't know what he was on that night, but he wasn't sober. He kept yelling at me and calling me 'Brenda.' That was Mom's name. You've probably guessed what came next. He raped me on the cracked linoleum of our living room floor. I was able to reach an empty bottle and hit him on the head. It knocked him out.

"I had been a virgin. He had taken my innocence. I thought he had taken everything from me at that moment, but it turned out that I was stronger than that. Stronger than him. I let it define me for years, but I refuse to give that filthy bastard another tear."

Mirren saw that most of the guests were moved—greatly moved—by Fiona's story. If Hannah Todd believed she could ruin Fiona with her hate, she would probably howl with rage from knowing that her viciousness had actually set Fiona free. Completely free.

"Finn got home and packed us up, and we ran. Our lives became the Campbell twins against the world—but we had our art, my brother and I.

"And then Mirren found me"—Fiona grinned at her—"and convinced the Smith Gallery to take a chance on me."

"Miss MacGregor didn't have to try very hard," Kain yelled out from the back, making several people laugh.

"I've since met the love of my life, and my hardheaded brother has fallen in love." She winked at Mirren, making everyone chuckle.

"Long story short, I was hurt badly by a man who should have loved and protected me. My brother is and has always been my hero and savior. I survived. We survived. We're both damn good artists. I admit that Ms. Todd was a bomb none of us saw coming, but I hope you will all forgive the interruption and enjoy the generous evening our patrons have graciously provided my brother and me.

"I don't want anyone to be uncomfortable around me. Ask me questions. Question my art. I implore you to rise above my past as I have.

"I was hurt, but I'm not a victim. Not anymore. I want you to see me in my art, and maybe, just maybe, Ms. Todd did me a favor. You know my story. You know *me*. I want you to know my art too.

"I paint street scenes that are real with real people. I see power and strength behind the mundane walks on a sidewalk, in joyful events as simple as a couple holding hands or a mother holding her child's hand, and even in the seedy meetings between drug dealers and buyers. I look at them and wonder what happened in their lives that made them choose those paths. People fascinate me. I hope they captivate you too. Look at my art and see yourselves."

And bless Jenson Paul, the young judge raised his refilled glass of champagne and said simply, "To art in its most honest form."

Fiona looked at her brother, and Finn looked back. The siblings wore mirror images of hope on their faces before breaking into wide grins.

Lyle, Mirren's uncle Coll, and her dad joined them. Her dad slapped Finn on the back, unnecessarily hard if Mirren were to judge, and patted Fiona on the shoulder gently.

"You two handled yourselves well," her dad began. Mirren could hear in his voice that he was moved by Fiona's story. "I'm proud of you both."

Unable to wait a minute longer, Lyle clasped Fiona to his chest in a bear hug, just holding her close and whispering in her ear. The scene even had her uncle Colly's eyes reddening.

Mirren grinned at Finn before telling her father, "Mom, Jo, and Aunt Cat will never forgive you and Uncle Coll for not letting them be here."

Her dad winced. "Jo will expect hours of meticulous recounting."

"Christ, have mercy," her uncle Coll prayed under his breath. "Lyle, you and Mir better bring your Campbells for a visit. Soon."

Mirren couldn't relax for long, listening to her family's banter. She still had a lot of work to do to encourage the Smiths' guests to mingle, and the judges still needed schmoozing—though, between Finn's and Fiona's extraordinary talent and Fiona's tragically heartfelt admission, the judges should have been putty in her hands.

The next hour and a half were long but exhilarating and satisfying all at once. Finn did not take his sister's sacrifice lightly. He quit lurking in the shadows and spoke with the guests and judges, even though Mirren knew he would have rather been at Alex and Sadie's pizzeria enjoying a whisky.

Mirren was dead on her feet by night's end but so pleased that neither her sore toes nor her drooping hair could lessen her happiness.

She finished seeing the last of the guests out. The judges had left thirty minutes earlier, along with the Smiths. May and Sloan had already been dismissed, leaving Finn, Fiona, Lyle, her dad, and her uncle Coll.

The evening had been an unquestionable success despite Hannah. Mirren still felt her face flush in anger when she thought of what that woman had attempted to do. Her nasty attack had been well beyond competitiveness. Hannah Todd needed professional help, and Mirren hoped she would receive it. If the police found that she was responsible for that artist's death...the woman needed to be put away for the rest of her life, mental illness or not.

One of the police officers had told Mirren that they would be investigating the incidents that had befallen several of the competitors. Lance had handed over all his research to the police that morning, but it looked as though Hannah was behind the events.

Forgiveness for the sick woman might come eventually, but that night was too soon to ask for absolution. Mirren was still cheering because the guests and judges had embraced Fiona. She had bared the darkest moment of her life to them, after all. It had been a joy to see the guests and judges go back to analyzing the Campbells' art.

Finn had withstood the handshakes and the older matrons bussing his cheek for being "such a good brother." Mirren had watched the man who had given her the worst first impression ever and found her body warming at his transformation.

He could have remained distant and taciturn as far as she was concerned. She was quite enamored with all Finn Campbell's idiosyncrasies. It was simply his nature, and she adored every one of his rough edges, but seeing him blush at the heaps of praise laid at his feet had made her chest explode with feeling.

Finn had made it clear that what they had begun was beyond dating. It was beyond hand-holding and sexy texts. It was a foundation. She trusted Finn as she trusted her mom and dad, which was absolutely.

Mirren closed the door and turned the locks before turning back to the room. She wouldn't go so far as to say it looked like a scene from a horror movie, but her family and friends were all silently watching her—in a very weird way. Mirren felt the hair on the back of her neck stand.

Fiona and Lyle smiled widely while the other three men looked on with grim expressions. A flush ruddied her skin from cheeks to chest at the bizarre attention.

Her steps faltered when she noticed her dad and uncle had their phones out like they were...videoing her. *What in the absolute hell?*

Forcing her feet to move, she closed the distance and asked, "Mind telling me what you nutters are up to?" Crickets. "Dad?" His smirk did little to reassure her. "Finn?" Her lover's blush and clenched jaw were not the reassurance she was looking for.

Finn finally moved and closed the distance between them. He cleared his throat nervously. "Finn?" she asked again. The funny business was suddenly ruining all the good vibes she'd been feeling. She frowned at all five "adults" in case they thought she was enjoying the...the pop-up flash mob drama.

Finn took her hand, causing a slew of nerves to kick off in her belly. She glanced over his shoulder at his sister, but Fiona only smiled and winked.

"Okay, now," Mirren started, past exasperated at everyone's odd behavior, "did you guys decide to take drugs while my back was turned? Because I can tell you...not a fan."

No one answered as Finn led her to his exhibit. He stood stiffly in front of his main piece. The woman's hand sculpture. Mirren would be lying if she didn't admit that when she'd finally seen the piece, her heart had felt like it might beat out of her chest. Had he created it with her in mind? She thought he might have. The ravens at the wrist were stunningly carved and surely not just a nod to the exhibit's name.

Each time Mirren's eyes flew over the sculpture, she found something new to admire. It was a bold showstopper full of softness and sensuality. It reminded her of a woman in repose, sated by a lover. She flitted her eyes to Finn. He left her that way.

The ring...well, the ring took her breath away. She wanted to ask him whether he had made the ring for the sculpture or the sculpture to showcase the ring. Why he had made it after their night together. What it meant. She hadn't. Her reticence in questioning him had left her flustered at her odd behavior. She questioned *everything*.

Finn looked at the hand for another silent minute, a severe air about his stiff shoulders.

When his eyes moved from the hand to Mirren, it was as though he was waiting, watching her with expectation. Her breath stuttered. Something was about to happen—something was happening already.

She noticed that their silent audience had followed them. Her dad's and her uncle Coll's recording was gratingly annoying. A part of her wanted to tell everyone to feel free to see their way out and definitely let the door hit them in the ass, but her mouth was dry and she feared her voice would come out all wobbly and unsure instead of witty and commanding.

"Have you figured out why I named this piece 4M+C?"

She swallowed deeply, praying to every salivary gland god. She had no help there, and her dry swallow became an exaggerated gulp. She finally managed an extremely intelligent "Umm..."

She had thought about its meaning. She'd pondered it about a thousand times before the fiasco with Hannah and then after. She just wasn't keen on voicing her conclusion. If she spoke it aloud and was wrong...there weren't words brutal enough to describe the ways in which she would want to die of embarrassment.

Finn dropped her hand so that he could trace the sculpture's palm. "Come on, Mir. You're far too intelligent to not have guessed. Tell me."

Wishing that they were alone but unwilling to back down because they weren't, she clasped her shaky hands at her back and answered. "The four *M*s stand for me. Mirren Mòr MacGregor-Morrow."

"And the *C*?"

"Campbell."

"I knew you'd get it," Finn praised. "From the moment Fi and I first moved in with you and I started working on this exhibit, and even during the many months we were apart, you have been my inspiration. The designs, the metal and stone colors—they all remind me of you."

He took both her hands and brought them to his chest. "My *Unkindness of Ravens* was always meant to find its way to you."

Mirren felt a lone tear slowly slide down her cheek. *Breathe, Mir. You don't know if this means what you think it means.* Finn was correct though. She was an intelligent woman, so she was pretty sure she knew where it was leading.

"*I* was meant to find my way to you."

With those nine words, Mirren knew...she knew for sure what all of it was about. What Finn was about to say.

He loved her as she loved him. It was fast, and many would think it was too soon, but she didn't care. They'd been separated far longer than they'd been together, but her heart had never stopped beating for him since the moment he'd irritated the hell out of her as soon as he'd opened his mouth. She could have done without the peanut gallery standing behind them because that level of romance was extraordinary.

Finn kissed both her hands and let them hang at her sides. She was tingling in anticipation of hearing the words, their audience completely forgotten. *I love you. I love you. I love you.*

But...Mirren was confused when Finn reached for his hand sculpture once more, plucked the stunning brown diamond ring from between its fingers, and—*Oh, Jesus*—kneeled on one knee.

When he took her left hand, Mirren noted that his hands were shaking as much as hers.

"I love you. Will you agree to marry me?"

It was simple, straightforward, no frills, and completely and utterly perfect. Stunned, she said, "I don't think I'm as smart as you think I am." At his questioning look, she went on. "I thought I knew what you were up to, but...I didn't."

He hesitated. "What is your answer, Mir?"

"Oh!" she gasped and rushed to admit, "You stole my heart months ago, Finn. Yes. Definitely yes."

Finn slid that gorgeous ring on her finger and stood, hugging her close and giving her a soft kiss on the lips.

He whispered in her ear, "I spoke to your dad first and asked his permission."

"I know."

That got his attention, and he pulled back, looking between her and her dad. "You knew?" he asked.

"If you'd asked me without Dad's permission, you two would be rolling around on the gallery floor, destroying art and tussling like two Six Nations rugby team rivals." She turned her head to her father and frowned. "Speaking of, why are Dad and Uncle Colly acting like social media influencers? They haven't stopped recording me this entire time."

Her uncle Coll simply said, "Cat."

Her dad said, "Your mom, Jo, and the Byrne sisters. It was either video your big moment or not give my consent to your... fiancé."

Mirren smirked at her dad's struggle with calling Finn her fiancé. She grinned at Finn. "You would have asked me anyway."

"I would have, but I wouldn't have liked the beating that came after." He grinned back.

Fiona joined them, giving out hugs and kisses and congratulations. "Who would have thought?" she asked, patting her brother's arm fondly.

"Not teenage us, that's for sure," Finn answered.

Finn hugged his sister, and they both whispered a few things to one another. Watching them together made Mirren's eyes sting with happy tears.

Who would have thought? Who would believe that a gift called *An Unkindness of Ravens*, of all things, had landed her the love of her life?

38

FOURTEEN YEARS AFTER THE CAMPBELL EXHIBITION—ROYAL EDINBURGH HOSPITAL

Redwood Ward, Room 11
Patient: Hannah Todd

"*Y*our *time is up, you dumb bitch.*"

"*Fourteen years, and you've managed* NOTHING*!*"

"That isn't true!" Hannah hissed.

"*Always and forever pathetic.*"

"*She'll never get us out of here. All these years of painting pretty landscapes and sucking off the therapist, and where has it gotten us?*"

"*In the same goddamn room, surrounded by the same pathetic losers!*"

"*I don't really mind getting the therapist's nuts off. He's disgustingly fat, and we have to flatten all the fat down around his tiny dick to get to it, but he's an easy fit, and he gets off fast. I like the candy he gives us after.*"

Hannah wanted to wretch over the picture the voice conjured. She hated Dr. Portman, and over the years, she'd thought of many ways she could kill him and make it look like an accident. She'd tried to resist, but her "companions" insisted she do it. They wanted the candy—humiliating her was a bonus.

She was painting alone in her room as far as the staff were concerned. A few years earlier, the hospital had finally relaxed their vigilance, believing Hannah was well and truly healed through medication or as healed as someone with "schizophrenia" could be. They never understood that her voices weren't an infliction. They guided her. Without them, Hannah would have been nothing. The doctors believed that the car crash she'd been in as a child had caused her to have "delusions." She'd never told them that they'd always been there.

Hannah kept a canvas up to make the staff believe she spent hours every day creating. In reality, she purposefully took a long time to complete anything so she could work on her real passion project: Mirren MacGregor Campbell.

Hannah had met Mirren only a handful of times, but the other woman had made it clear that she didn't like Hannah. The bitch had some weird taste since her BFF was an incestuous weirdo. Had Fiona not been in the competition, Hannah wouldn't have had to resort to unsavory tactics, and she definitely would have won a place in the museum. It hadn't been surprising to find out Mirren had also been screwing the brother. Talk about special treatment.

Hannah was convinced that if Mirren had never been involved, she wouldn't have had to do all the things that had ended her up in that damn hospital.

"Jesus, the idiot is still working on her Mirren scrapbook."

"A lot of good it's done us so far. Years obsessing about one woman instead of finding a way to get us out of here."

"She's always been a selfish whore."

"She's old, fat, and ugly now."

"Yeah, she probably doesn't want to get out of here. Maybe she figured out she'll be just as embarrassing outside as in."

"*Sucking a fat man's cock for candy is all she can hope for at this point.*"

"Shut up. All of you, just SHUT UP!" Hannah winced, hating when the voices drove her to speak to them out loud. If she were caught, all her years of hard work would have been for nothing.

She'd never had any visitors. Her mother gave her an allowance but never set foot in the hospital. The uncaring bitch had made a full recovery, according to an article written by her dear brother, Lance.

She had a laptop, and even though it had a gazillion restrictions, she could look up the news and do research on the Campbell Cunt—she preferred that moniker to "Mirren." She'd saved her allowance for months for a printer and fun scrapbooking stuff. Scrapbooking helped her pass the time between therapy sessions and medication schedules. Ever since she'd been allowed computer access, Hannah had looked up hundreds of art-related queries a day. After months, she was able to swing an occasional browse into the gallery manager's personal life without drawing attention.

She flipped through the colorful pages, smiling at the photos of Mirren. Social media was a grand place to connect with the bitch's family and friends. Glancing at the clock on the wall, she quickly tucked her book away on a secret shelf hidden under her art desk before the afternoon meds nurse entered.

Hannah smiled at the heavy cardboard shelf she'd created from the thick box her printer had come in. Tying it up had been a pain in the ass, but macramé weaving created great hangers. Arts and crafts were encouraged at the Royal Edinburgh Hospital.

She had barely put away the book and picked up a paintbrush when the nurse walked in. Hannah smiled kindly at her. "Afternoon, Deirdra. I hope your day wasn't as brutal as it sounded." A new patient had been admitted and screamed to high heaven for hours.

Nurse Deirdra sighed and rolled her eyes as she gave Hannah her little cup of pills. "The Lord knows I'm going to need a bottle of wine tonight to make my head stop ringing. That poor lass is in quite a way." Deirdra shook her head in sadness.

"Stabbed her professor with a pair of scissors," she gossiped. Either Deirdra hadn't looked through Hannah's file, or she'd managed to forget that Hannah had slashed a man's wrists and watched him bleed out. But, sure, stabbing a teacher with some Fiskars shears was practically the same thing.

Hannah placed the paper cup to her lips and tossed back the cocktail of antipsychotic meds, opening her mouth and moving her tongue around as she'd been doing for years to prove she'd swallowed her meds.

She tapped her paintbrush against the wooden easel, smiled at the nurse, and said, "It might make your day brighter to know that I've almost got your daughter's birthday present finished." Hannah hid her disgusted grimace at the peaceful small land-scape where she'd made a herd of horses into colorful unicorns. Deirdra's daughter was turning six and obsessed with the horned beasts.

The nurse gushed and praised the painting and Hannah's skills before she remembered she had at least ten more patients to drug up. The moment the door closed, Hannah stood.

"Hurry up, Hannah."

"Puke your guts up already."

Hannah didn't hesitate to go to her personal bathroom, where she immediately bent over the toilet and stuck two fingers down her throat. It had taken a long time for the staff to allow her private bathroom privileges, but thanks to good old Dr. Port-man, Hannah had more leniency than other patients.

There had been a year or so when she'd actually taken the meds, making the voices so quiet she could barely hear them. She'd hated it. Hated being separated. She knew the voices were unfair and vicious, but they were all she had left.

"Christ, clean yourself up. You make me sick to look at."

"How did you get so ugly?"

"It isn't fair to make us look at you every day."

"This place was amusing for a few years, but we're done, Hannah. Do something, you pathetic piece of shit!"

Hannah stared at herself in the bathroom mirror, contemplating whether or not to tell them what she'd been working on. Deciding the time was right, she raised her eyebrows and let a wide grin spread across her face, feeling smug and proud and everything wonderful for the first time since she'd been thrown in that place by her bitch of a mother and left to rot.

"You know the recording device I saved up for three years to buy?" Hannah could feel the silent aggression swirling around her brain. Before the voices could taunt or mock her, she went on. "I don't just video my painting classes for YouTube."

Silence. And then...

"You clever, clever whore."

"You've been holding out on us, Hannah. I approve."

"Who knew Dr. Portman's miniature wiener would be our ticket to freedom?"

"Finally, Hannah, you've done something worthwhile."

Hannah preened as she grinned at the grinning image in the mirror. Nothing, absolutely nothing, was better than when her voices approved of her.

A few more weeks of creating content, and she would have enough blackmail to force the doctor to finally release her from that place. She had so many things to do. So many things to see.

So many people to destroy.

Truth be told, she had only one target. That person was a

budding artist, talented and beautiful. She was also related to Mirren MacGregor Campbell, who was related to Finn Campbell, who was related to Daddy's Little Pet, Fiona Campbell.

"Soon. Soon. Soon."

39

FIFTEEN YEARS AFTER THE CAMPBELL EXHIBITION, THREE WOLVES DISTILLERY— IRELAND

Bébhinn Byrne-Dunn's 90th Birthday

R aven stood side by side with her sisters, River and Rowan, watching the antics of their family and friends. They were raucous and reckless and messy and everything wonderful. Usually, their husbands were the recipients of the three sisters' attention, but at that moment, it was the large group of children that held their gazes.

All the kids, teenagers, and young adults mingling was quite a sight. Their laughter made every adult watching them smile.

Almost everyone had been able to make it to the party celebrating her nan. Lyle and Fiona hadn't, though, and were greatly missed. Their twelve-year-old son, Kenin, was a scientific genius, and their family was at the 3M Young Scientist Challenge in the United States. Mirren and Finn were on pins and needles waiting to see how their nephew would place.

Raven smiled at Dean and Mary, Mirren and Finn's ten-year-old twins, named after their O'Connor grandparents. Mary had cried for weeks after their names had been revealed and rarely let her great-grandchildren out of her sight.

247

Obviously, her son and her sisters' children were there, as well as Gray MacGregor, Thomas (Honey Bunny to those who wished to keep it old school) and Josephine's daughter, who was about to celebrate her nineteenth birthday. Gray was a stunner, just like her mother, in a green wrap dress. Their son, Lochlann, was also present. The fifteen-year-old was the spitting image of his father, big, blond, and moody.

Coll Bar and his wife, Catriona, who was also Thomas's sister, had made it with their two children, Blair, who was seventeen, and Laith, who was fifteen and the spitting image of his father too. Loch and Laith were inseparable. Jo and Cat said it was like seeing an echo of their husbands.

Charles Morrow and his wife, Aileen, Thomas's ex-wife and Mirren's mother, had brought their youngest daughter, Margaret—or Mags, as she was lovingly called—and the sauciest young lady Raven had ever encountered, definitely in her sister River's league. Mags was eighteen, outspoken, beautiful, and so sincerely sweet that everyone on the receiving end of her blunt tongue forgave her instantly.

Bébhinn, Gray, Blair, and Mags were best friends, and watching them interact reminded Raven so much of her and her sisters as teenagers. They were still like that, if she were being honest. The two girls in the group whom Daniel and Jonathan had invited as dates were being soundly ignored. That was no surprise, as the quartet rarely approved of her and River's boys showing interest in girls. Rowan's daughter, Bébhinn, always sided with her best friends over her brothers.

Glancing at her sisters, Raven nodded toward her son, Daniel. "How is my little, tiny baby twenty-one?"

River snorted. "How is Nan ninety? How are we in our forties? Why do I now look at nonsurgical spa services like an à la carte dessert menu?" Then she sighed and admitted, "It's hard sometimes to see our kids grown. Jonathan is twenty, but I swear I still hear his giggles when the house is quiet."

"And look at Bébhinn!" Rowan motioned toward her daughter with the hand that was holding a personalized Glencairn crystal whisky glass. The fading sunlight was filtering through the renovated stable windows, making the etched O'Faolain Three Wolves logo glow warm and golden against the whisky. "Doesn't she look the mirror of us at that age?"

"Spitting image, Row," River agreed.

"Watching our children grow together has been"—Raven hesitated—"well, it's meant everything to me. They have each other, like we had each other."

"Yes," River said with an uncharacteristic softness to her voice. "And like Bran and Patrick had Hugh."

As if speaking their names made them appear, their husbands joined them, each man wrapping an arm around his wife. Bran and Patrick still had stunning white hair, with only a few shadowy pieces around their temples. Laugh lines might have creased their eyes and smiles a bit more deeply, but to their wives, they were more handsome then than when the brothers had swept Raven and River off their feet.

At seventy-five, Hugh, the patriarch of the O'Faolain clan and husband to her youngest sister, still had his steely glare, gruff attitude, and absolute devotion to his wife. Rowan still sighed when he walked into a room and grossed his sons out by discussing her sexcapades with their father. Much to everyone's amusement, Hugh's hair had turned as white as his boys'. Hugh had never stopped being a gym junkie, so his body was still incredibly fit, though he had lost the bulky muscles of his youth.

Bran leaned down to kiss the side of Raven's neck, telling her, "Pat and I got Nan settled in her room. She told us at least thirty times that tonight was her best birthday ever."

"Oh, I'm so glad. Nan tires fast these days." Several guests were staying overnight at the Three Wolves Distillery. There were several rooms available at the distillery's event venue. Raven and her sisters were so proud of their husbands' success. Their Three Wolves whisky had blown up worldwide, becoming a coveted brand for both casual drinkers and connoisseurs. The event venue always had a waiting list for everything from weddings to mogul weekend retreats.

Out of all the O'Faolain business ventures, Three Wolves was the one all three brothers' children were interested in most, which pleased the older O'Faolain men to no end.

"You fucking pansies got to escort Bébhinn to her room," Hugh groused. "I had to walk that old dragon, Diana Graves, and her 'friend,' Evan Dunn. Christ, the woman berated me for the entirety of the trek. Everything from my failure as a man to my 'dramatic personality' and 'poor parenting' was laid on my shoulders."

Rowan hugged Hugh and kissed his chest. "She misses your mother. Putting you through a tongue lashing is her way of saying she loves you."

Matilda O'Faolain had passed away a few years before. She was still missed terribly by the family. Hugh had buried his mother next to his father, Jonathan, in Tulsa, Oklahoma, where his family had lived for many years.

Bran shuddered. "If that's Diana's love language, I don't want to know what her disapproval looks like."

Mirren and Finn Campbell joined their group of six. Fifteen years earlier, the Campbell twins had taken over Europe's art scene. Finn's jewelry and sculptures were so coveted, he and Mirren had had to move to a country fortress further outside Edinburgh just to stop reporters and rabid brides begging for his one-of-a-kind wedding bands from camping out on their property.

His twin and her husband had moved with them, of course. The two siblings didn't want to ever be too far apart. Raven understood and approved. After all, she and her sisters and their husbands had renovated a four-story building in downtown Dublin to live in so they could be close.

"If it isn't Smith Gallery's top talent finder and money maker." Rowan grinned at Mirren as she accepted a glass of Three Wolves.

"You forgot to include Mir's fancy artist sidepiece, Row," River teased.

"Glad you could make it, Campbell." Bran shook Finn's hand while Patrick thumped his back.

Her father-in-law didn't greet either of them except for dipping his chin. Twenty years hadn't changed that man since the sisters had first met him in Oklahoma. "What a great day, right? Mary and Dean look to be having a fine time." Raven glanced at the twins playing the popular American game cornhole with several other kids. "You'll never get them to settle tonight. I think I've seen them sample the chocolate fountain about fifty times."

"Their Grandma Mary pretends not to see her great-grandchildren doing anything naughty." Finn chuckled.

"That woman lets them get away with everything. No surprise. She did give birth to Josephine." Mirren shook her head in exasperation.

Mirren's lips suddenly rounded, and a high-pitched squeal came out. Josephine had come up behind her stepdaughter and pinched her butt.

"Mirren's telling tales again." Jo grinned, joining the group. Thomas stood sentinel at her side. He did give his oldest daughter a soft smile.

"Jo, damn it! You're lucky I didn't pee my pants. You'll

remember this body dropped twins," Mirren sniffed, pretending offense.

"Ten years ago, Mir. Let it go already," Jo answered with a grin.

"You're terrible." Mirren grinned back. "Which reminds me. Loch is being the biggest grouch tonight."

"Stop trying to hug him the moment you see him, and I imagine he'll get over his grumbles," Jo advised.

"He's huggable though. I want to hug him, and I will, and he'll damn well take it," Mirren insisted.

"Singing to the choir, Mir." River chuckled. "Daniel and Jonathan acted like Raven and I were the second coming of a plague when they were that age. They got better, I swear."

"Because Hugh 'spoke' to them," Rowan added, miming air quotes.

Raven hid her smile when Hugh's cheeks turned pink. "Hugh knew it hurt our feelings. He's a fixer." Hugh glanced her way and winked.

"Is it really bothering you, Mir?"

"Not really, I guess," she admitted, elbowing Finn in the side when he snorted in disbelief. "Fine. A little. I don't get to see him very often, so when I do, I want a damn hug."

"Lochlann," Thomas growled just loud enough for his deep voice to reach his son.

Every eye in the place, including his son's, zeroed in on him. Mirren's whispered "Dad, for the love of God, I didn't mean for you to say something this second!" went unheeded.

Thomas's mini-me carefully and slowly joined his father. When the two MacGregors stood shoulder to shoulder, Lochlann stood silently, waiting for his dad to speak. Raven had to hold her breath so a giggle didn't escape as she watched Mirren's face turn bright red.

Gray joined her brother and sister, raising her brows at her older sister, curious about what Mirren might be up to. Mirren shook her head from side to side, closing her eyes. She was probably dying of mortification because she was about to get called out for tattling at thirty-six.

Without a single muscle in his face altering, Thomas told his son, "When your sisters want a hug, you'll do it with no complaint. Is that understood?"

Lochlann's eyes bulged, and scarlet swept across his neck and cheeks. He glanced over his right shoulder to where his best friend was valiantly trying to suppress his laughter. Lochlann's "Yes" sounded more like a question than acquiescence.

Mirren shrugged off her embarrassment and looked at Gray and grinned. They weren't about to waste the opportunity to stick it to the baby of the family. The sisters stormed their brother, giving him big hugs and his cheeks smacking kisses. Smart boy that Loch was, he took the love without complaint and even managed a few pats on his sisters' backs.

Like Raven had thought earlier, their family was wonderfully messy. When Laith's guffaws became louder, his father, Coll, was there to flick his ear, making Lochlann chuckle. Those boys were messes.

Mags sauntered over, her lovely brown-black waves trailing down her back. Blair followed, her stunning, barely restrained red curls swirling about her tiny body; she was even more beautiful than her mother, which Raven would have sworn was impossible. Catriona was a stunner. Blair was ethereal. Jonathan and Daniel brought up the rear, leaving their dates behind. Clearly, the older kids were drawn to the drama.

Mags narrowed her eyes at Laith, making the teenage boy's eyes round—no one wanted on Margaret Morrow's bad side. "Since we're airing the family particulars, Laith won't hug any of us girls, even his own sister," she said, to which Blair, who was hearing impaired, signed, "Shut your piehole, Mags."

Finn nudged his wife, Mirren. "This is all on you. You know that, right?"

"God, I know. Christ, how I know. This family is—"

Finn finished Mirren's thought. "Extra."

"So extra," Mirren agreed, "though fun for all that." Raven and her sisters laughed at Thomas's oldest daughter. Always a shit stirrer.

Raven watched Coll look to his wife, Catriona, who was wearing a resigned look, to his daughter, Blair, who signed a quick "Don't," and to his son, Laith, who definitely wasn't laughing anymore.

There wasn't one parent there who wasn't protective of their children, but Raven believed that because Blair was deaf, Coll was just that little bit extra.

Seeing his father's disapproval, Laith quickly kissed and hugged his mother, then his sister, and then Mouthy Mags, Gray, and Bébhinn. Coll still said, "Don't make me address this again," to which Laith replied, "Of course, Da."

Crisis averted, the party resumed, the kids drifting away from the adults. Raven didn't blame them. She did hear Lochlann lean close to his sister, Mirren, and say, "What the hell, Mir Mir?"

She whispered back, "I miss you."

When her eyes blinked rapidly with emotion, it took all of three seconds for her little—Raven used that term figuratively—brother to bend and give her a quick peck on the cheek before whispering, "I'll do better, Sis," and then sauntering off to rejoin his best friend.

Bran spun Raven around and pulled her to his chest, gently kissing her lips. "I love you."

"I love you. Always." After running her thumb gently over her husband's lower lip, she turned to her sisters, who instinctively turned toward Raven. They clasped hands and smiled at each other.

"We have a pretty incredible family," Raven stated.

"I'm thankful every day," River said solemnly.

"I pray it never changes," Rowan added.

All good things must come to an end.

> — GEOFFREY CHAUCER, TROILUS AND
> CRISEYDE (3.615)

ALSO BY ANNE GREGOR

The Scottish Lions

Josephine

Catriona

Mirren

The Irish Wolves Trilogy

Raven

River

Rowan

ABOUT THE AUTHOR

Anne Gregor has a Master of Arts in History with a Civil War emphasis. For her thesis, she focused on Irish immigrants working the transcontinental railroad across America, specifically those who settled in Oklahoma amongst Native Americans. A love for research turned into a love for fictional writing, and soon, every old document Anne studied became the premise for a novel. Though Oklahoma remains near and dear to her heart as she lives on Grand Lake O' the Cherokees, she enjoys traveling the world with her characters. **Anne is the author of two contemporary romance series, The Irish Wolves and The Scottish Lions.**

www.ingramcontent.com/pod-product-compliance
Lightning Source LLC
Chambersburg PA
CBHW020418110726
47899CB00006B/2034